18501

ENTER A PLACE WHERE ORDINARY PEOPLE COMMIT EXTRAORDINARY ACTS— AND THE PUNISHMENT DOESN'T ALWAYS FIT THE CRIME

- A woman returns to her girlhood home to dig up a decades-old secret
- A man who daydreams of bereavement devises a foolproof scheme to kill his wife
- A psychic spooks a woman who's plotting a brazen historical theft
- An old-time movie star has sinister plans for the bestselling writer who slashed her in print
- A lonely little girl, a resourceful sleuth, and a young man with an unusual method for remembering are all involved in a bizarre mystery in a compost heap

Nevada Barr

PRESENTS

MALICE DOMESTIC 10

AN ANTHOLOGY OF ORIGINAL
TRADITIONAL MYSTERY STORIES

AVON BOOKS
An Imprint of HarperCollinsPublishers

AVON BOOKS
An Imprint of HarperCollins*Publishers*
10 East 53rd Street
New York, New York 10022-5299

First Avon Books paperback printing: March 2001

Avon Trademark Reg. U.S. Pat. Off. and in Other Countries, Marca Registrada, Hecho en U.S.A.
HarperCollins® is a trademark of HarperCollins Publishers Inc.

Printed in the U.S.A.

10 9 8 7 6 5 4 3 2 1

Contents

CONTENTS

Nevada Barr, whose mysteries feature park ranger Anna Pigeon, won an Agatha Award for her first book in the series, Track of the Cat *(1993). Her most recent Pigeon novel is* Deep South, *which reflects Barr's move to Mississippi in the early 1990s. She talks here about the rich banquet of choices for readers of Malice Domestic mysteries.*

Introduction:
An Immeasurable Feast

Nevada Barr

To remain alive means to change. The mystery has not only remained alive since Wilkie Collins introduced the genre in the nineteenth century, but has continued to grow and flourish until now mysteries command a lion's share of readers' hearts. Every form of literature is said to have a "Golden Age." This is arguably the golden age of mysteries. Neither readers nor writers can be satisfied with the simplicity of *whodunnit*. The stories have become ever more complex, depending on a sense of place, the psychology of the characters, the strengths and weaknesses of humanity pushed to the extreme by what still remains our most heinous of crimes—the taking of another human life.

It's been said there are only seven mystery plots in the world. I tend to think this is a generous assertion. Somebody dies, somebody did it. In a traditional mystery, where the myriad insanities of the mentally deranged serial killer are not in the offing, the motives for human evil are limited: the perpetrator wants to get something or somebody, keep something or somebody, hide something or somebody, or be revenged because one of the above was denied. With this palate of very human emotions, writers continue to surprise, inspire, and amaze. It is not the crime that keeps the mystery on our night table, but the ever-changing and continually fascinating study of the human condition.

Short stories, like poetry, are asked to do these things in few words. All the ingredients of a novel are in a good short story. Over the years, many have been successfully expanded into movies and books because the richness was there to begin with. But the story, the short story, requires a writer with the skill to pack the necessary goods into a small space. It also requires a reader with imagination to take the clues and the images and, with her mind, bring to them the depth of a world.

For ten years Malice Domestic has been a forum for this discipline. To create a puzzle that teases, an ending that satisfies, a universe that is at the same time familiar and believable yet challenging and unique, in only a few pages is a daunting task. With a plethora of other entertainments available to us, amusements that do not ask much of us as audience members, I believe the short story is an ever more important training ground for writers and exercise yard for readers.

My love of short stories stems not only from the intense satisfaction I derive as a reader given a mental conundrum that I cannot solve and seeing it solved in such a way I laugh at myself and say, "Of course," but from the small window the short story format opens into the minds of other writers.

The sheer length of a novel allows for meandering, philosophizing, the leisure to create a sufficient amount of smoke and mirrors that one's shortcomings in plot or character can be obscured. Not so the short story. It is a perfect collaboration between author and audience. Skill or lack thereof cannot be disguised with word play.

The tremendous popularity of the mystery novel has made it difficult to sort the good from the bad without spending a lot of money and time. There is so much to choose from. Besides simply having fun with short story anthologies, they serve me as a shopping guide. Because a writer can write a splendid short story doesn't mean he or she can write a splendid novel, but it certainly suggests the possibility. Many authors whom I now await with eagerness and actually buy in hardback, I discovered between the covers of a Malice Domestic anthology.

Malice has taken the time and effort to collect the talents of some of our better known writers—all Agatha Award nominees or winners, as well as some who very well may be in the future. It's a dim sum of mystery that can be consumed by those as greedy as myself in a delicious afternoon.

So, without keeping you any longer from just such a wonderful repast, I introduce *Malice Domestic 10*.

A resident of Seattle, K. K. Beck has written suspense nov-
els (Unwanted Attentions), *historical mysteries* (Mrs.
Cavendish and the Kaiser's Men), *thrillers* (Bad Neighbors), *and humorous whodunnits* (The Body in the Corn-
flakes, The Revenge of Kali-Ra). *She was nominated for
Agatha Awards for her short stories "Rule of Law" and "A
Romance in the Rockies," the latter featuring flapper sleuth
Iris Cooper, who also appeared in* Death in a Deck Chair,
Murder in a Mummy Case, *and* Peril Under the Palms. *In
this story, Iris investigates a legacy of Italian paintings to a
mysterious beneficiary.*

The Tell-Tale Tattoo

K. K. Beck

Portland, Oregon, seems like an odd choice for
someone looking for a place to die, but that is what I believe Miss Spencer chose to do. I first heard about her in a
letter from my Aunt Hermione.

April 1928
Portland, Oregon

Dear Iris,

Our neighbor Professor Poindexter has finally gone off to the Amazon on that expedition in search of giant spiders he has been planning for so long. I pray he does not bring any live specimens back with him! Mrs. Poindexter will accompany him. She is such a devoted wife. What a shame that her husband's specialty shouldn't be something more pleasant. Butterflies, for instance. In any case, they have rented their house, furnished, to a lady from back East.

Mrs. Poindexter introduced her to me before she left. Miss Spencer is living alone with a maid she brought with her and has hired a woman to do the cooking. She told me she had come here to be near her only living relative, a nephew who I take it is trying to set up some sort of business here about which she seemed rather vague.

She appears to have spent a great deal of time in Europe, where a lot of her relatives tragically died all at once in an avalanche. They were from Boston and had something to do with railroads. Miss Spencer has brought with her only the things she loves most: a magnificent collection of Italian pictures, and a few books and things. Iris, I do believe she is not well. She is very thin and tires easily. Still, there is a strange serenity about her, rather like one of the sadder but resigned Madonnas among her wonderful paintings. She is about thirty-five or so, and handsome in a haggard sort of way, with pale skin and a cloud of soft, light brown hair.

There is, I feel, some sad story in her life—apart from the fact that she may be suffering from some serious illness. I have been perhaps friendlier than I usually would be with a new neighbor because she seems lonely. I will be very interested in your impression of her.

I smiled when I read the letter. Aunt Hermione had managed, with her usual efficiency, to find out a great deal about Miss Spencer. When I came home for my summer vacation from Stanford, my aunt and I paid a call on her. While there was indeed a brave sort of languor about Miss Spencer, she became very animated when I asked about her pictures. I particularly admired a small, square portrait of a young Venetian woman of the Renaissance period with wavy pale gold hair and a pearl necklace.

"It is one of my favorites," she said, touching the ornate gilt frame. "Not a Titian, but almost certainly from his *scuola.*" She looked at me thoughtfully and said, "She has that Titian red hair, just like you, Miss Cooper, and she is probably about your age." I blushed and said I hoped I hadn't admired the picture just because of that, and she laughed quite merrily. It was a nice throaty laugh, and suddenly she seemed much younger and more vigorous, and I realized that she must have once been quite lively. How sad that her poor health had robbed her of her true nature.

As we were sitting down to tea, the maid, a trim French woman, came in and said that Mr. Spencer had arrived.

"My nephew," she said to us. "Always dropping in unexpectedly. My late brother's boy, Sidney. I'm really just getting to know him. He ran away from his prep school and ended up out West somehow." She smiled indulgently. "He's rather high-spirited, as I was when young." One of her brows arched, giving her a suddenly jaunty air. "My family didn't want me to run off to France during the Great War to become a Red Cross nurse either."

I was glad that she had something of the same temperament of her only living relative. So many people have a slew of relatives and nothing in common with any of them.

A young man with brilliantined hair came into the room. He was dressed for the links in plus fours and a scarlet and yellow argyle sweater with matching socks. "Hiya, Aunt Edna!" he said heartily. After brief introductions, he refused to join us for tea. "No, I'm in a hurry. I just stopped by to see how you are and to let you know I'm having a fella come over and appraise these paintings. For the insurance, you know. I know how crazy you are about 'em, and if anything happened to 'em I know you'd be heartbroken." He grinned happily at the walls and gave her a wink. I had the impression he had been drinking.

Miss Spencer sat up a little straighter. "These pictures mean a great deal to me," she said, "but I don't see what having them appraised for their monetary value has to do with my feelings about them."

"Of course not, of course not," said Sidney hastily. "I just wanted to make sure your affairs were all in good order." There was a little silence, and he added nervously, "I'm only thinking of you. Well, never mind, then. Is there anything else I can do for you?"

"I don't think so, Sidney," said Miss Spencer with a narrow-eyed, thin-lipped look.

"Say, listen," he went on breezily, "you wouldn't happen to have a little moolah on you, would you? I seem to have left my wallet at home, and I'll need something to tip the caddy with. I'll square it away with you next time I see you."

"How careless of you, Sidney," she said with a forced little laugh. "Please excuse me, ladies." As she left the room with Sidney in tow, presumably in search of her handbag, Aunt Hermione and I exchanged glances. How sad that Miss Spencer's only relative should be such an oaf. And, as her only relative and presumably sole heir, it was pretty tactless of him to take such an obvious interest in the cash value of what might someday be his while the present owner was still alive.

About a week later, Mrs. Jones, the lady who does our ironing, told us that her sister Muriel, who is a friend of Miss Spencer's cook, reported that Sidney and Miss Spencer had had an unpleasant conversation, in which Miss Spencer had been heard to say loudly: "I'm afraid you have been a great disappointment to me, Sidney."

A few days later Miss Spencer asked Aunt Hermione to recommend a lawyer. "She specifically said she wanted someone who could do a will," reported Aunt Hermione with relish. "I gave her Mr. Musselwhite's name."

In the coming months we saw a good deal of Miss Spencer. She seemed quite happy to see us, but in a quiet, distracted way. She spent a lot of time in her rose garden, which was particularly lovely that June. By late July, however, she was frail and weak, and although nothing was ever said, it was clear she was very ill indeed. The doctor came often, but of Sidney, there was no sign. Near the end, I read to her—Browning, Keats, and Shelley was what she wanted to hear.

She died in August while we were away at Lake Oswego, and when we returned, I was astonished to learn from Mr. Musselwhite, the lawyer Aunt Hermione had recommended and an old family friend, that she had left me the picture of the young Venetian woman. As a legatee, I also received a copy of the will, and its contents were fascinating. I read it in Mr. Musselwhite's office downtown.

The will was handwritten, and Mr. Musselwhite told me he had not drafted it, but that it was properly witnessed and perfectly legal. Miss Spencer had simply given it to him for safekeeping and asked him to probate it for her.

The will didn't mention Sidney at all. A large bequest went to her maid. The rest of her estate, including the paintings, went to someone named "Captain Reginald Montague of the Royal 21st Barsetshire Fusiliers, who shared my love of Art and of Life, as it can be, but so seldom is, lived." She had underlined "lived" three times. She had also elaborated. "Though Reggie and I had just that one glorious month together in the spring of 1915 before his wounds healed and he rejoined his regiment, it was a month that lasted a lifetime. I cannot believe that any two people could ever have experienced such intense love in every meaning of the word as we did during those few short weeks. Only he and I will ever know what there was between us."

At least until now, I thought. I was absolutely thrilled with Miss Spencer's indiscreet will. Knowing that she had had a past and had really lived made her short life seem so much less tragic. I saw a younger Miss Spencer in her crisp uniform, giving her arm to a tall, clean-limbed Englishman in a maroon silk dressing gown and walking him around the leafy grounds of the hospital. In his cool gray eyes lay the sadness of knowing he would soon be back at the front, perhaps to die. And if he was to die, she must have reasoned, surely there was no reason to hold back.

Mr. Musselwhite must have seen my eyes glowing as I read this, for he clicked his tongue and said, "I am sorry I have to show one of your tender years such a document. I would never have advised Miss Spencer to reveal her most intimate feelings. Nor would I have encouraged her to reward some foreign cad, who, it appears, took advantage of an innocent American girl. But I was not consulted."

I wondered what had kept them apart after the war. It must have been something awfully big to thwart such a deep love. Were they promised to others? Maybe he had died in battle. This thought caused me to ask Mr. Musselwhite sharply, "What happens if Reggie isn't alive?"

"Then her nephew Sidney gets everything," he replied. "Except for your picture and the bequest to the maid." He shook his head sadly. "Had I drafted the will, I would have suggested she name a residual legatee. I am not sure she intended her nephew to inherit." Mr. Musselwhite sighed. "But perhaps it is for the best. I don't believe in cutting out relatives on a mere whim or caprice. Especially when there is a family fortune of many generations standing. The ties of blood are surely more important than a brief, sordid, youthful attachment, however intense." He glanced up at me, looking embarrassed, and coughed, no doubt thinking he had been too frank with a young girl.

"I hope Reggie's alive," I said defiantly. Reggie wouldn't, I felt sure, care about mere money, although as a sensitive man who loved art I'm sure he would love the pictures as she had. The thrilling part, however, was that now he would know how much she had loved him. Perhaps that knowledge could sustain him throughout the rest of his life.

"I'll try to find him," said Mr. Musselwhite dubiously. "His old regiment seems to have lost track of him. Some misunderstanding about mess funds. Apparently, he left England. He could be anywhere. I've advertised in the English papers to see if anyone knows where he is."

"We've got to find him!" I said.

Mr. Musselwhite sighed. "I'll do my best. Meanwhile, I wonder if you and your aunt could do me a kindness."

"What is it?"

"Well, Miss Spencer's maid seems pretty overwhelmed, and her English is poor. We need to get the effects in order. The lease will be up on the house soon, and everything must be packed away. I will see about proper storage of the paintings, but there are clothes to be gone through, that sort of thing. It needs a woman's touch.

"It wouldn't be right to have Sidney Spencer go through the effects, as he's not mentioned in the will, but as the likely heir, he has expressed concern that if these matters aren't taken care of, the estate will be liable for rent beyond the terms of the lease."

Sidney seemed pretty smug about getting his hands on everything. Mr. Musselwhite had probably encouraged him. He'd practically come right out and said he should have inherited. Reggie had to be found!

As I left Mr. Musselwhite's office, I figured out just how he could be found sooner rather than later. I went directly to the Western Union office and wired my friend Jack Clancy, a reporter for the *San Francisco Globe*. Back home, an hour later, a long distance operator announced there was a call from San Francisco. I grabbed the telephone and told Jack all about the missing heir.

"Pretty hot stuff," he said appreciatively. " 'On her deathbed, lonely heiress reveals her one moment of happiness. Their forbidden love blossomed as the world went mad. Where is Reginald Montague now? Did he spill his blood on the fields of Flanders, his last thoughts of the pert little American nurse who had brought him back to health and life? Or is he alive, a lonely man whose youthful spirits were crushed by the horrors he saw around him in the trenches?' "

"That's the ticket!" I said enthusiastically. "But I don't think Miss Spencer was ever *pert,* exactly. She was more pale and interesting."

Jack continued his story in a sad but indignant voice. " 'Where is Reginald Montague now? Will he have learned too late how much she cared for him? Is he alone and friendless, lamenting his lost youth and lost love?' "

"I hope we can find him," I said. "The poor man."

Jack switched offhandedly to his regular speaking voice. "Reginald Montague probably has a wife and five little Montagues by now."

"How can you be so cynical?" I asked indignantly.

Jack laughed. "We'll find out soon enough if enough papers pick this one up. Think we can get a picture of either of them?"

"I'll find out," I said, delighted that Mr. Musselwhite had asked me to go through Miss Spencer's things.

I didn't find any photographs next door, but I found something else that proved to be quite useful. While Aunt Hermione and Miss Spencer's weeping maid, Yvonne, went through her closets and laid her clothes out on the bed to give to charity, I went through the small shelf of books. When I had read to her, I saw a small, blue cloth-bound book on the shelf, and it had aroused my curiosity. Examining it now, I saw that it was a diary covering the war years. Flipping through the entries for 1915, I found this:

Captain Montague—I call him Reggie now when we are alone—is so much better. Really, he is incredibly frisky and energetic, fairly bursting with vigor. I can scarcely keep up with him. His recovery has been astonishing. What cruel irony! I have nursed him back to health, and given him all the cheer and comfort I could, only so that he can be sent out again to the trenches. But we never speak of it. We live only for those sweet, stolen moments behind the sheet cupboard or in the shed at the back of the garden. It came up just once when I ran my fingers lightly over the tattoo on his right arm—his regimental crest with its moving motto—Valor and Fidelity—beneath it. The very qualities which he embodies! "It wasn't my idea," he said, glancing down at his arm. "The CO suggested we all get one. Makes it easier to sort out

*the bodies on the battlefield." "Oh Reggie!" I said.
"Please don't even speak of it," and fell weeping on
his manly chest. "Buck up, old thing," he said. "No
need to be gloomy. Let's enjoy ourselves while we
can."*

It was a few days later when Mr. Musselwhite called.
"Are you responsible for the story that ran in the *Oregonian* this morning?" he asked.

"Well, I guess I am," I said. He sounded annoyed. I had
only been trying to help.

"I wish you'd told me. Sidney Spencer is hopping mad.
He says this kind of publicity will bring out all kinds of
charlatans and impostors and we'll have a devil of a time
sorting them out. He may be right."

"It won't be too difficult," I replied with a certain feeling
of triumph. "I happen to know that the real Reginald Montague has a tattoo of his regimental crest and motto on his
right arm." I explained about the diary, and described the
tattoo in detail. Mr. Musselwhite seemed to be taking
notes.

A week later Mr. Musselwhite called and asked me to
come to his office immediately with the diary. "Two Reginald Montagues have made an appointment to see me this
afternoon," he explained. "One of them wired me last week
and arrived by train from Vancouver, British Columbia,
this morning. The other telephoned me this morning. I'd
like to have a copy of the description of that tattoo. That
should stop any charlatan in his tracks."

When I arrived at his office, slightly out of breath and
very excited, I saw two men in the waiting room eyeing
each other warily. They both looked to be in their mid-thirties. One was tall and bald with a fresh pink complexion. He wore a well-tailored suit with a white camellia in
his buttonhole and a red and white striped tie. There was a

monocle on a black silk cord around his neck. The other was shorter and stouter. He had a small reddish mustache and a slightly rakish air due to the fact that he had a light overcoat draped over his shoulders like a cape. He too wore a red and white striped tie. I tried not to stare at them.

Mr. Musselwhite's secretary, a severe-looking woman in a black dress, with steel-gray hair in neat waves, rose and said, "Mr. Musselwhite will see all of you now." We followed her into the office, where Mr. Musselwhite was sitting behind his desk. To my surprise, Miss Spencer's nephew Sidney lolled in a nearby chair, a worried expression on his face.

"Captain Montague?" said Mr. Musselwhite.

"Yes?" they both said.

Mr. Musselwhite sighed. "Gentlemen—and I use the term advisedly, as at least one of you must be an impostor—would you be good enough to roll up your right sleeves and show us your right forearm."

"Certainly," said the bald man in a plummy English accent. He removed his jacket and began fiddling with a cuff link.

"This man is an impostor!" said the man with the mustache. "This is an outrage." He turned to the bald man. "Who *are* you, sir!"

"Why I am Captain Reginald Montague," said the bald man. He was rolling up his shirtsleeve calmly as he spoke. "I imagine you're looking for the old regimental tattoo," he said to Mr. Musselwhite. "Stag couchant on a field of red, with crossed white bars."

"Iris, would you please find the passage you told me about in the diary," said Mr. Musselwhite. He turned to the other man. "This is all very unpleasant but I believe we can save a lot of time if you would please show me your right arm."

"I can't do that," said the man with the mustache, shedding his coat with a flourish. "I left my right arm at the Somme!" Indeed, the sleeve of his tweed coat lay flat and was neatly tucked into the pocket.

The bald man held up his arm triumphantly. "There it is," he said, looking down at a tattoo. "And our old motto. Words to live by." I looked down at his arm. There it was, all right, in capital letters: VALOR. FIDELITY.

"The motto was in Latin," said the man with the gingery mustache irritably. "Virtus, Fidelitas. That's what my tattoo said. I believe you are an impostor, and furthermore that you were never even in the Royal 21st Barsetshire Fusiliers at all! You have no right to wear that tattoo, or that necktie!"

"But the diary said Valor and Fidelity," said Sidney. "Surely we have to pay attention to what it says in Aunt Edna's diary."

"Oh," said the bald man with a look of great sadness. "Was Edna your aunt? Let me offer you my deepest sympathy. She was a wonderful woman." His eyes glazed a little. "A remarkable woman. So full of life and vitality."

"How dare you speak of Edna in that familiar way?" said the other Captain Montague.

"I think she translated the motto when she wrote it down in her diary," I said. "But even if it *had* been in English, it would not have been spelled without a U. That's the American way. In England it's spelled V-A-L-O-U-R. I imagine you got this tattoo this week, right here in Portland. Soon after Sidney Spencer heard from Mr. Musselwhite that a Reginald Montague was arriving from Canada. It will be easy enough to find out, I imagine. Just a matter of the police asking a few questions at tattoo parlors."

The bald man stared in horror at his forearm. I turned to Mr. Musselwhite. "The tattoo wasn't mentioned in the newspaper stories. I found out about it after I talked to my reporter friend. And I know you told Mr. Spencer here about it, because he just acknowledged as much by saying the motto was in English. Did you tell anyone else?"

Mr. Musselwhite glared at Sidney. So did the bald man, who said in a different accent entirely, without a trace of Englishness, "You stupid idiot. Now I've got to wear this stupid tattoo for the rest of my life!"

"At least you will have your right arm, which is more than the brave Captain Montague has," said Musselwhite angrily. "Get out of my office, both of you! In fact, why don't you both get out of town? We don't need riffraff like you around here. If you don't, I will call the police."

"Here is my passport," said Captain Montague briskly after they had departed hastily. "I also have some of her letters and a photograph of her." He handed them over to Mr. Musselwhite. "Poor Edna," he said sadly. "Had she no other relatives?"

"A lot of them died in an avalanche," I explained.

"And she never married? I always assumed that she was a wife. There was some boy in Boston her family expected her to marry. If I had only known she was here, and alone," he said sadly.

"Did you ever see her after the war?" I asked. I had to know.

"I wasn't myself after the war," he replied. "I was feeling pretty low. Lost my bearings. Didn't want her to see me maimed like this. And there was her immense wealth! Why would she have wanted half a man—and a poor one?" He sighed.

"I got to know her in her last days," I said. "I believe that she faced her death bravely. She didn't seem to be alone. She had her pictures, which she adored. And poetry. And some very happy memories." I handed him the diary.

Mystery writer, playwright, and a past BBC radio and tele-vision producer, the versatile Simon Brett was toastmaster at Malice Domestic III and guest of honor at Malice XII. Author of numerous mystery works, including the novels featuring struggling actor/sleuth Charles Paris and the widow Melita Pargeter, Brett was nominated for an Agatha Award for his short story, "Heavenly Bodies," and for an Edgar Award for his rollicking Malice Domestic 6 *short story, "Ways to Kill a Cat." In this tale, Brett chooses a most unusual narrator: a £10 note with an attitude.*

A Note of Note

Simon Brett

I like being in leather. Good leather. It has a very nice smell, classy, relaxed, affluent. And that day I started in ex-tremely good leather.

I was in an expensive wallet. Probably, with farm prices the way they are these days, it cost its owner more than the animal who sacrificed a small patch of hide to make the thing.

The wallet was, of course, no less than my due. Notes of my class never boast about their breeding, but because there may be common people perusing this account of my day (I gather the target audience is mystery readers—yeugh!), I will make an exception. I may look like the rest, with the Queen on my front and Charles Dickens on my back, but in fact . . . I'm a tenner with a Double One Serial Number. (I should make it clear at this point that genuine currency aristocrats have no problem with the word "tenner"; it's only the parvenus and nouveaux riches who insist on calling themselves "ten pound notes" all the time.)

Anyway, as notes of my background know, but rarely mention in polite society—and I'm only mentioning it now because I'm not quite sure whether all mystery readers belong to polite society—Serial Numbers with a Double One in them are the crème de la crème. The face of the Queen on my front definitely smiles more benignly on my Serial Number than she does on those of the common herd.

I'll tell you, incidentally—because I'm in such a generous mood—that the digits of my Serial Number are 26011015, which of course provides me with that very exclusive central distinction. Having a Double One with exactly three digits on either side—as those of you who read such tabloid rags as *Royal Mint Monthly* will no doubt be aware—puts me at a very rarefied height of the banknote nobility.

Those of you who're hoping that I may also reveal the two-letter prefix to my digits must, I'm afraid, go whistle. There are some levels of Bad Form to which I will not stoop, least of all for a mystery-reading audience.

I have to confess that this time yesterday I was in a cashpoint. You may think that such an experience might be demeaning for someone of my breeding, but I can assure you it's something we all go through. Just as human aristocrats have to suffer the standard nine months in the womb and the humiliation of childbirth before taking their rightful place in society, so we of the currency peerage must endure the humiliations of printing, stacking, and, with increasing frequency these days, loading into what is vulgarly known as a "hole in the wall."

At least I was with my own kind. Inevitably, as a Double One Serial Number fresh from the Royal Mint, I was surrounded by other Double One Serial Numbers. Just as human aristocrats all go to the same kind of schools and universities, so we too in the early parts of our lives stick to our own kind.

And, as a rule, Double One Serial Numbers don't talk in a cashpoint. You'll hear a bit of raucous badinage from the lower-class notes, but almost nothing from our lot. Maybe, when we're actually being withdrawn, one of us may say a terse, "Well, I'm off—good luck, chaps!" but that's about it. Double One Serial Numbers instinctively understand the value of the Stiff Upper Lip.

Because, of course, it is a tense moment when you're actually taken out of the "hole in the wall." Bit of a lottery. You have no guarantee that your breeding will be matched by that of the person withdrawing you. And they're allowing all kinds of riffraff to have cash cards these days.

Still, I was lucky when I was drawn out yesterday. The omens were good. Late evening withdrawal, and he took out twenty of us. I was safely in the middle of the pack, surrounded by other Double One Serial Numbers—none, obviously, of quite such elevated breeding as I was, but at least my sort of notes.

And as soon as I smelled that leather, I knew I'd landed on my feet. I had been withdrawn by someone of the utmost breeding and distinction. It was appropriate.

(I should mention here that the social accolade to which all notes aspire is unfortunately one that can never be realized. The ultimate validation of one's status would be residence in the handbag of that lady whose impression we so proudly bear on our frontage. But, sadly, Her Majesty the Queen never carries any money.)

So, anyway, I spent last night in a fitting environment for one of my rank. Surrounded by my peers, in expensive leather, and crisp. (For a note, the duty of keeping oneself crisp cannot be overestimated.)

I was even more impressed the following morning when the wallet containing me was removed from the trousers (charcoal wool and cashmere mix with the discreetest of pinstripes) that had been cast onto a chair the night before, and replaced in the back pocket of another pair of trousers (paler merino wool in Prince of Wales checks). And the switch wasn't done by the owner of the trousers, but by his valet, who laid out the suit with his master's other clothes.

I was in the wallet of a man with staff. Yes, I was in my proper milieu.

His breakfast was served by a cook, which was another very good sign. The buttocks on one side of the wallet that contained me felt reassuringly opulent, and the ridge of the chair that pressed on the other side had the authentic feel of Chippendale.

After breakfast I was presented with more evidence of my owner's wealth and status. When he left the front door of his house, he was welcomed into his car by a uniformed chauffeur. (You may wonder how I know, from the fastness of my expensive leather wallet, that the man was uniformed. Let me tell you, someone of my breeding can tell that kind of thing just from the sound of a subordinate's voice.) And the lush leather upholstery against which I was pushed left me in no doubt that the car was a Bentley.

The car came to a halt. "Bond Street, sir," said the chauffeur in a voice indicating that the badge at the center of his peaked cap was very highly polished.

The door clicked open, and my owner eased his ample

buttocks off the soft leather. "Thank you, Wilkins." I approved of this. It doesn't hurt members of our class to be civil. Other people are quite sufficiently aware of their inferiority without our rubbing it in.

As my owner strolled nonchalantly along Bond Street, I did have a moment's misgiving. Not about him—I could not have wished to end up in better company—but about his relationship with money.

Someone of his undoubted wealth and status would surely do everything by account or Platinum charge card. He would very rarely use actual notes, but—and this is what brought something of a chill to my watermark—when he did use them, it would mostly be for tipping.

Oh dear. I did not relish ending up in the sweaty grasp of some hotel doorman, maître d', or taxi driver. Having landed so firmly on my feet, I had no wish to start slumming.

But even as the thought threatened, came reassurance. I would be safe. Someone as well-heeled as my owner would never be so mean as to tip with a tenner. It was the twenties who would have to watch out for the greasy paws of the gratuity hunters. (And, to my mind, that wasn't a bad thing. Twenties don't have anything like the class or rich ancestry of us tenners. They're bigger and flashier than we are and, it has to be said, they reek of New Money.)

No, I would be all right.

Fatal thought. Had I realized how much I was tempting providence, I would never have had it. Because, even as relief flooded my pulp, I had a sudden shock.

I was jolted and heavily compressed as the buttocks of my owner struck the pavement. And, simultaneously, I heard a rough voice shout, "Keep still, or I'll kick your bloody head in!"

My owner was unceremoniously pulled over onto his front, and from his back pocket I felt the wallet ripped out.

He had been mugged! By someone common!

Just how common the criminal was soon became clear. His grubby hand snatched out me and my crisp, flat peers—and threw the wallet away. Clearly we were dealing with someone who had no appreciation of beautiful things.

I and the others were roughly folded and thrust into . . . I'm sorry, I still go slightly trembly at the recollection.

No, I must be brave and just come out with it. We were thrust in and zipped into the inside pocket of . . . a nylon *anorak*. There—I've said the word.

And then the mugger took off, running at great speed. From the traffic noise and the sounds of shouting around him, he was clearly moving toward a less salubrious part of town.

I have to confess I was in a terrible state of shock. And I wasn't the only one. Although the notes around me did not have natures quite as sensitive as my own, they were still Double One Serial Numbers, so they were not without feelings. But nobody said a word. I think that's a tribute to the way we had been brought up.

I heard the quack of Chinese voices, which suggested we might be in the Soho area, and then suddenly the traffic noise and shouting grew quieter and was swamped by the sound of heavy footsteps running upstairs. The mugger had gone inside a building.

I heard knocking on a door, which after a while opened. An elderly woman's voice of distinctly proletarian origin demanded, "What do you want?"

And our captor, whose accent also lacked the gloss given by the right sort of school, replied, "You know what I want. Gaynor in?"

Apparently Gaynor was. As the mugger moved through the flat, my senses were assaulted by cheap music and cheap perfume. A door opened and closed. A female voice,

of fewer years but no more breeding, said, "Oh, it's you
again. Can't get enough, can you?"

"That's my business. I'm the one who's paying."

"So long as you've got the money, see if I care."

"I got the money all right."

With that, a hand was thrust into our temporary nylon
shelter, and the whole folded pack of us was pulled out into
the dingy light of a vulgarly draped bedroom.

And then . . . I would advise any readers of a nervous
disposition to skip the next paragraph.

And then, ten of our number were unceremoniously
peeled away from the others, rolled up into a cylinder and
thrust . . . The very recollection turns me as pale as my
watermark. But I must persevere. We were thrust into a
woman's cleavage! Yes, into the little niche between the
spangled front of her brassiere and the clammy flesh of her
stridently scented breasts. Ugh! For that to happen to a
Double One Serial Number! Was ever humiliation so
deep?

All right. Those of a nervous disposition may start reading again now.

But to those of you of a prurient disposition, I say forget
it. If you think I'm going to describe the scene that ensued
in that sordid bedroom, forget it very firmly indeed. You're
meant to be readers of mystery fiction, for heaven's sake. If
it's porn you're after, then you should change your reading
habits.

Suffice it to say, then, that within twenty minutes I and
my deeply shocked fellow notes had taken up residence in
a whore's purse. We were crumpled and jumbled up in
there with a squalid riffraff of lesser notes and extremely
uncultured coins, not to mention keys, condoms, grubby
lipsticks, and other repellent female impedimenta. Let me
tell you, it wasn't just this girl's morals that needed tidying
up. It was everything about her life.

A couple of hours passed. They were filled with other sordid carnal transactions which I have no intention of detailing. Then suddenly the purse that contained me was picked up as Gaynor left her bedroom.

"Where you going, then?" It was the voice of the older woman, presumably her maid.

"Get some stuff," the girl replied.

"You're meant to be working. If Big Phil hears you've been taking time out—"

"Shut up!" And the outer door was opened and slammed.

Gaynor went out into the street, but didn't go far before turning into another building. The rough conversation, Muzak, and acrid smell of beer suggested that it was a pub. Oh no! I wasn't going to have to slum in a till behind a bar, was I? That would be too, too demeaning.

But it wasn't a drink she was after. She sat down at a table and said, "Hi."

"What do you want?" asked a surprisingly civilized voice.

"Looking for my friend Charlie, aren't I?"

"I'm afraid Charlie's like a cheap supermodel, love. Doesn't get out of bed for under fifty."

"I got money."

There was the sound of a zip opening, and light flooded into my squalid quarters. Gaynor's hand thrust in and grabbed the bundle of notes that included me.

I wasn't about to enter the possession of a drug dealer, was I? That would be even more mortifying than being in a pub's cash register.

But luck was on my side. I lay number six in the stack of ten notes with which our mugger had paid for the girl's services, and it was the five above me who were peeled off and became statistics of the country's illegal drugs trade. I allowed myself a fleeting moment of pity for their fate, but my main feeling was one of huge relief.

It would not have been so huge had I known the fate that awaited me back at the girl's flat. I lay curled up in her purse, in squalid surroundings certainly, but with the warm glow of having had a narrow escape. I might have lost a little of my crispness, but at least my dignity remained intact.

Even as I had the thought, the zip sounded again, and I was snatched from my temporary haven. And then . . .

I still shudder to contemplate what happened then.

The girl rolled me up into a tight cylinder and stuffed me up her nose.

Presumably, being a nice class of mystery reader—as you undoubtedly are—you have never suffered the ignominy of being shoved up a human nostril. And if you know what's good for you, you'll keep things that way.

However, since it is my self-imposed task to give an account of my day, I must not flinch from describing the experience to you.

It was horrible! If you have any illusions that the female nostril is a smooth shell-like receptacle, dismiss them. It is a hairy damp orifice, and the fluids that make it damp do not bear contemplation. Imagine a note of my pedigree being tainted by mucus!

Nor was that the end of my ordeal. While one end of my rolled self was buried in snot, the other was positioned over a thin line of white powder, which the girl proceeded to snort. Oh, the shame! That a Double One Serial Number like me should be employed as a conduit or siphon for illegal substances!

Beside that destiny, even mixing with the louche company of a pub till becomes an attractive proposition.

My current owner did not, however, have long to enjoy any high the cocaine might have given her. Hardly had she finished snorting than the door of her bedroom crashed open.

"You little cow!" bellowed a coarse voice of foreign origin. "That's my profits you're shoving up your nose! I'm going to have to teach you, Gaynor, that you give all the money you get straight to me!"

"No, Phil, don't hit me!" she screamed.

If you think that I'm going to describe what then ensued, once again you're out of luck. There is no more room for violence in my narrative than there is for sex. You're meant to be the kind of reader who enjoys nice cozy mysteries, with very little blood and satisfying moral resolutions. If you want anything more racy, I suggest you close this book immediately and pick up something more suited to your depraved tastes.

Some half hour later I, along with every other note yielded by his ransacking of the flat, had taken up residence in Big Phil's wallet. Nothing, I fear to say, like the elegant leather one in which I had started my day. The pimp's wallet was leather-look plastic, cracking at the seams, and the other notes in it were a motley selection, all grubby, some torn, and one or two even mended with strips of transparent tape. Hardly appropriate company for a Double One Serial Number.

Though I'm afraid I was no longer the smart, flat, crisp note who had started the day. I had lost my sheen of newness. I had been crumpled and rolled. One of my long edges was still damp and smelly with mucus, while the other bore a few grains of cocaine. I was undoubtedly in reduced circumstances.

But the ability to endure adversity is a feature of good breeding, so I said nothing. Complaint could only be a sign of weakness, and I did not wish to show myself up in the presence of the lower orders. There must be some purpose in this suffering, I reassured myself. It will make me a better banknote, and I will appreciate all the more my good fortune when I am restored to my proper place in the currency hierarchy. I am a tenner born to be worshiped, not humiliated.

My next move, however, made clear to me that my tribulations were not yet at an end. Big Phil reached for his wallet as he walked into a building redolent of cigarette smoke and male sweat. A tinny commentary could be heard. "And as they go over the water jump, this favorite's holding back in third, but looming ever closer to the front-running . . ."

Yeugh! I was in a betting shop. The torments visited upon Job began to look rather appealing, compared to the day that I was being put through.

Big Phil turned out to be a man of quick—though not necessarily wise—decision. Taking all the notes out of his pocket, he assembled a sheaf that included me and totaled one hundred pounds. Then he scribbled a betting slip and approached the counter. "I'll take that thirty-three to one on Sloppy Joe." And we were thrust across the counter to an impassive girl who smelled of throat sweets. She separated us by denomination and laid us down under sprung wires in the trays of her till.

Be grateful that you have never had to endure the smell of the inside of a betting shop cash register. Heaven knows whence its denizens draw their amalgam of scents, but let me tell you, the level of P.O. (Paper Odor) is quite appalling. Even worse than in those fabled sinks of noxiousness, pub tills.

I lay on top of the pile of tens, which position might be thought a suitable recognition of my status, but which was not without its drawbacks. For a start, I had been put in facedown, and the restraining wire was pressing very hard on the nose of my Charles Dickens. Then also, of course, hot air rises, and the sweaty P.O. from the notes beneath me was quite disgusting.

Big Phil's interest in my future was abruptly curtailed.

Sloppy Joe lived up to his name by unseating his jockey at the first fence.

And I was left in my malodorous prison, my fate dependent on the vagaries of four-legged animals. A big win, and who knew in what pocket I might end up?

But no, the gods had not yet finished with me. They had planned another cruel twist in my fate.

Suddenly, there was a commotion in the betting shop. There were screams, and a rough voice shouted, "Give me all the money you've got in your till!"

I got a fleeting whiff of throat sweets as the girl behind the counter—suddenly less impassive—opened the till and scrabbled to extract me and my nifty companions from the trays. We were shuffled together into a rough pile, with me still on top, grabbed by a man with a stocking mask over his face and thrust into the inside pocket of a leather jacket. Not good leather, I fear. This smelled as if it had just come out of the tannery.

"All right, nobody move!"

Somebody must have moved, though. I heard the sound and felt the recoil of the shotgun as it was fired. There was a truncated grunt of pain, and then someone screamed.

"Anyone else try anything and they'll get the same!"

Nobody else did try anything. The robber moved gingerly out of the betting shop. In the background a racing commentary continued, unaware of the fact that it had lost everyone's attention.

As soon as my new owner got onto the street, he burst into a run. In the nick of time. There was the sound of a police siren.

"Bloody hell!" His running got even faster. Inside his pocket, I was the one nearest to his chest, and I could feel the frantic pounding of his heart.

"Get out of my way!"

This instruction clearly wasn't heeded, because there

was a juddering blast from the second barrel of the shot-gun. A cry of pain was heard.

Then the street noise died, as the thief—and now possibly murderer—went inside another building. He closed the door behind him and gasped as he tried to regain the rhythm of his breathing. His heart was fluttering against me like a trapped bird.

He reached into another pocket of his jacket. From the clicking noises, I deduced that what he'd taken out were cartridges to reload the shotgun.

He froze at a sound from outside. The metallic voice of a loud hailer called, "We know you're in there, McDade. Leave your weapon and come out with your hands up."

"Like hell," he muttered.

"Do as we say, McDade, or it'll be the worse for you."

He was silent. The loud hailer persisted. "McDade, you can't get out of there. We've got police marksmen covering the door. Come out, leaving your weapon inside, and with your hands up, or we'll come in and get you!"

"Oh yes?" he murmured. "I don't think so. Make more sense to me if I come out and *get you!*"

As he spoke, I heard the sound of a door thrust open, followed almost immediately by the Dickens-shaking impact of two shotgun barrels being fired.

But there were more than two bangs, and the reason McDade rocked backward was not just the recoil from his own gun. I felt the impact, as a bullet ripped through the stack of notes in his pocket and made a neat hole above the Queen's right eye.

That was the absolute end! Never mind the harm it had done to me, I regarded the perforation of our ruler as a blatant act of lese-majesté. Committed by a member of her own police force too.

I didn't have time to pursue this thought, as I suddenly found myself immersed in sticky fluid.

Oh no! McDade actually had the nerve to bleed over me.

Really! The day was just going from bad to worse. I should never have come out of that cashpoint.

Breeding will out, however. Though that day was a complete disaster, it did have the effect of getting me the recognition that was my due.

(And I'm sure you're glad about that. Mystery readers, I know, like happy endings. The wicked are punished and the good triumph. That's the appeal of the cozy, isn't it?)

McDade, it turned out, was a notorious criminal whom the police had been after for years. He was already wanted for eleven murders, before the two he committed while I was in his possession.

So the police cornering and shooting him dead was a very big news story indeed.

And I became an extremely famous tenner. People come and look at me almost every day, and I've gotten used to their gasps of awe and admiration when they see me.

I still carry the bullet hole, and the blood has now dried to a rust color, but those who care about the finer things can still read my serial number and recognize that it's a Double One. Not that they need to, of course. In spite of my wound and the bloodstains, they can tell I'm something rather special in the currency world. As I say, breeding will always out.

So I reckon, really, that all this homage is no more than my due. I think I deserve to be in this glass case in the Black Museum at Scotland Yard.

Though I'm not sure I'd have chosen the caption "The Tenner That Couldn't Save McDade."

*Susan Dunlap lives in Berkeley, California, and has writ-
ten seventeen novels featuring former forensic pathologist
Kiernan O'Shaughnessy, police officer Jill Smith, and me-
ter reader Vejay Haskell. She was an Agatha nominee and
Anthony winner for Best Short Story for "Checkout," and
also was nominated for an Agatha for her story, "A Con-
test Fit for a Queen." In this story, Dunlap's enterprising
house sitter encounters some unexpected difficulties in her
job . . .*

People Who Sit in Glass Houses

Susan Dunlap

Melanie Beckworth paused in the doorway. The
morning sun glinted off her shiny, exquisitely styled blond
hair, her pale beige cashmere dress, her pale leather shoes
and suitcases. She looked so perfect here in her magnificent glass-walled house, I almost expected the sky to
blacken and a loud voice from above to order: "Stay home,
Melanie." But it was Melanie herself who spoke. She eyed
me as she would something smeared on her shoe. Then she

picked up her bags and left me with these words: "There have been three burglaries on this block alone. Be especially careful not to leave the doors unlocked, Ginger."

I should have followed her advice to the letter instead of adopting my *serious house sitter* expression and consigning her warning to the back of my mind. If I had . . . Well, *had I but known*, right? What I did was nod slowly and let a moment pass—a client likes to think her house sitter is intent on memorizing her every instruction. Then I smiled reassuringly. "Your house will be safer with me here than it is when you're at work all day."

Her narrow lips hadn't quite parted. She probably didn't even realize she was about to protest. But I could see I'd gone too far. It offended her to think her house could be safer with a stranger than her own self. I might as well have called her a bad insurance risk. Most people have a decent, considerate relationship with their house sitter, but I could tell Melanie Beckworth viewed me as only slightly less of a threat to house and home than leaving same unoccupied. When she'd seen me walk into her white-on-white living room, me in my orange turtleneck and navy sweatpants, I thought she was going to declare, "Empty house danger be damned," and shove me back out the door.

Before she could speak, I assured her, "I'll keep careful watch, doors locked even when I take out the garbage, outside lights on by dusk. I'll only be gone to do errands and to walk Barney." At that, a shaggy little black and white Tibetan terrier jumped up against my thigh and I scratched his cute little head. He was the icing on the cake of this house-sit—twenty-five pounds of lick and cuddle. I love dogs, and that's a big plus with their owners. But I could tell it wasn't quite enough for Melanie Beckworth, so I added, "I'm staying in the most intriguing house in the neighborhood. With these glass walls, I can sit in the living room and look out on the park. I can sit at the dining room table and look out at a stream. I can look out at trees on every side. Why would I want to be anywhere else?"

I was afraid I'd overdone that, but Melanie Beckworth nodded in the same way she would have had I said the driveway leads to the garage.

It *was* a gorgeous house, and as soon as she drove her BMW convertible out of the driveway I gave Barney a "pig's ear," a rawhide chew a good bit larger than his own ear. He set to work on it in a way that said it was a bigger treat than he was used to getting without performing. I smiled. It was good for the household dog to think of me as an indulgent; it made him less likely to roam. I loved the way he held the pig's ear between his paws and tore into it as if nothing else in the world mattered.

Then I made myself a cup of tea and retraced the route Melanie had chosen to take me on the tour. I wanted to decide how much of this luxurious abode I could put to my own use without worrying about a scene if Melanie should come home early. Homeowners are pleased to hire a reliable stranger to be in their house, it's just the idea of that woman "living" in it that gives them the creeps. I'm careful, but even I can't always predict what will set them off. One woman didn't care about me sleeping in her bed, but had a fit when she discovered I'd chosen the blue flowered cup for my tea. Needless to say, *her* house is taking its chances with burglars this year.

And just as well. It was hardly a match for Melanie Beckworth's. This house was a long rectangle, floor-to-ceiling glass set on a slab over the carport. Like a giant shoe box with its end facing the park across the street. (Of course I would have swallowed my tongue before saying that to Melanie Beckworth. *Half a million* and *shoe box* are not terms meant to be together.) The living room spread across the front and L'ed back into a dining area from which I could see the creek. The kitchen formed the other quarter of that square. Behind were two bathrooms, two bedrooms, and the stairs down to the garage and guest room. The hot tub was in back. This was, after all, California. Melanie had suggested I would like the privacy of the downstairs guest room, the one that looked out on the carport.

Melanie was wrong.

I liked *her* room, with its king-sized bed, the view of the waterfall in back, the morning sun that would pet my face before I was fully awake. I loved the master bathroom with its kidney-shaped black Jacuzzi, low and wide, just begging to have a glass of merlot on its generous rim. With its magnificent sound system, its superb lighting. I could have skipped the bedroom and lived in the bath.

Perhaps if I had been thinking of it, her warning would have guided me away from the master bedroom where a burglar might assume the occupant slept. But by this time that bit of "paranoia" was no more pressing to me than her note over the kitchen faucet: "Do not let this drip." (As if I'd be more likely to notice the sign than the dripping!) No, it was my professionalism that shaped my decision. I live in a studio apartment on the fifth floor rear of a featureless building downtown. It's cheap and a perfectly adequate little cell in which to stash myself between jobs, but I don't want to do any more time there than I have to. And to pay even the rent for that, I need these jobs. Not to mention the chance to be with dogs like Barney. It's hard enough for a middle-aged woman on the edge, but owning a dog screws every transaction up a notch. A safe, cheap studio that allows dogs is a dream. If I did find one, I would worry constantly that my dog would offend the landlord, eat the molding, or, God forbid, bark. But when you house-sit, it's not your dog who chews or barks. And generally, a dog that's a terror normally can be quite the little gentleman when his owner's not around to go crazy at each bark. For me, these two weeks were going to be a well-paid vacation. I wanted nothing to stand in the way of Melanie having me back next year, and of referring me to her friends.

I didn't want to presume.

Let me be more accurate here. I didn't want to be discovered presuming.

So I didn't presume to sleep in Melanie's room. But I did take the other upstairs bedroom, which Melanie used as an office. She had an office in the bank she worked for in San Francisco, and I doubted she "banked" at home on weekends, but what else was she going to do with this room? Such a problem, too many rooms. This one had a day bed that would get the same morning sun, plus one of those teak corner desks that goes along two walls. On the desk sat a computer, two in-boxes—empty—and the kind of desk sets people get only as gifts. Over it was a picture that screamed, "Safe behind me!" I confirmed that. Well, you do. Just like you look in the cabinets and anyplace else likely to hide something. A house sitter too *un*curious to bother with that would hardly be worth having in the house. I mean, we are employed to watch out for things.

I plunked down my suitcase to unpack later. "Want to go for a walk, Barney?" I called.

I took the terrier's answer to be yes.

And so began our routine. Three walks a day for him, add errands for me, and true to my word I was "home" the rest of the time. The trick of house-sitting is to ride the edge of presumption without falling over it. Presuming it's my house. Why else would you take the job? When I first started house-sitting I was terrified I'd fray the edge of the oldest, thinnest hand towel or chip one of the everyday dishes in the dishwasher. But I've evolved. Now when I step out of the hot tub I wrap myself in the five-star bath

sheet. At dinner, the good sterling clinks against the fine
china. But I'm careful; what I use, I put back, and in exactly the same spot. I do it right away so there's no last
minute panic or chance of mistake. I don't take chances.

Well, only one, and maybe it's that titillating toe-over-
the-edge that switches the roles of owner and servant to
host and tourist.

Each morning I lifted a book-sized, soft, pale leather
jewelry box out from the back of Melanie's underwear
drawer. Why she had chosen to hide it there, covered only
by lacy teddies, I couldn't say. She was not a trusting
woman. Maybe she had no choice. The safe in the other
room was small, and most likely it was already crammed
with financial papers and other jewelry I'm hardly a safe-
cracker, still, it took me less than a minute to wriggle a
wire in the little lock and open the box. If she'd left the box
unlocked, I would have given its contents the cursory
glance I gave every cupboard. It was its being hidden and
locked against me that gave the rings and bracelets inside
their power. This early morning moment was the finest of
the day. I picked up a sapphire ring or a diamond bracelet,
held it up and let the sunlight sparkle off the stones. I
turned it sideways and assessed the effect. Over the years, I
had established rules for this all-important moment:

First, no necklaces, for two reasons. Practically, they
were too noticeable. What if a neighbor came to the door
and saw a pendant with a ruby surrounded by a spray of diamonds hanging over my sweatshirt? How could she *not*
mention it to my employer? And aesthetically, the times I
would notice it myself were too limited. How often do you
look at your own chest?

Second, no piece of jewelry could be worn more than
once; to do so would suggest mundanity.

And finally, the decision had to be made before I put the
piece on my finger or wrist. I never wanted to hold up my

hand with an amethyst set in a gold band, decide against it
and then have to come back to it on a later, and thus lesser,
day.

So I'd make my choice, slip it on wrist or finger—I have
small fingers and any woman's ring will fit one of them—
and let it take me by surprise each time I turned the page of
the morning paper. By the afternoons, I'd become almost
used to it as I worked on embroidery. Providing unique
pieces to dressmakers is how I keep myself in food. It's an
odd livelihood, forever endangered by imports and changing tastes. It's the one marketable skill I have from my hip-
pie years. And by now I have connections on all levels of
the handmade rag trade. From two to four P.M. I'd curl up
in the white high-backed overstuffed chair by the living
room window and look out at the park between stitches,
and then the sun would play on the gem from a different
angle and the piece would make my breath catch all over
again. Around four P.M. the fog began rolling in, and soon
the sun was slicing over its edge, thin and sharp as a hand-
tooled cleaver. In it, the gem virtually danced and the shine
of its gold or silver setting cut at my eyes. There was no
way I could work. Each afternoon I sat dead still, just looking at the marvel of art and nature much longer than I
should have. Then, regretfully, I swiveled the chair around
so that the tall back shielded me.

I don't know what Melanie did on the weekends, but I
kept the shades up all the time, even at night. Before dinner, the last ray of sun behind the fog and the live oaks in
the park was too lovely to miss. So what if people looked
in and saw me—that's the point of a house sitter, isn't it?
They could hardly miss me—a comment I'm sure Melanie
would be making to her vacationmates. I was the only
thing in the room that wasn't white. Well, Barney and me.
I guess Tibetan terriers don't come in all-white. I was
tempted to eat dinner in that living room chair, but again, I

have rules. I can eat on my lap at home. (Actually, there, I have to.) Here I must dine in the dining room on the fine china, with candlelight and music. Then it's a bit of reading, a phone call or two, Barney's last walk, and off to lounge in the hot tub or the Jacuzzi. I didn't wear the jewelry into the tub, but I left the ritual of returning it to Melanie's jewelry box as the finale of the day. Carefully, I placed it back exactly as she left it, locked the box, and returned it to the closet, or in this case the underwear drawer.

All day I'd play CDs, and as loud as I chose. I liked to discover my host's favorite music and devote myself to it—a sort of minicourse in Shostakovich or Sibelius. Having spent time and money on his collection, my host would have the widest selection, performed by the best orchestra, and usually played over a sound system to rival Symphony Hall. I've ushered a couple times for the symphony, so I appreciate good music, and prone is definitely the position in which to hear it.

Melanie's house had amazing acoustics. It was like having the entire orchestra follow you from room to room. Outside, the only hint of music was a soft buzz. Of course, if you were listening for it you could hear it, but otherwise you'd never notice. I marveled at that the time I forgot to turn the sound system off when I went to the hot tub and came back in to the last movement of the symphony. Even so, the next night when I stretched out in the wonderful black Jacuzzi, alone in this house whose amazing glass walls blocked Shostakovich, I didn't think of burglars or my screams bouncing off the glass unheard.

I did think of the burglar the day before my stint was over. I thought about him precisely at 4:22. Not the middle of the night, 4:22 in the afternoon. I had just made myself a cup of hot water. (I thought later perhaps if I'd made tea, the burglar would have caught a whiff and been warned someone was home. But I'd made the hot water because this was my last day and I had restocked Melanie's tea cabinet and I wanted to leave it untouched.) So I set my cup on the coaster next to the high-backed chair, plunked myself in the chair and reached for my book. At that point three things happened. Barney jumped up on my lap, I knocked over the cup, and I felt a breeze. I didn't connect the breeze to the door opening, not immediately. I was focused on getting a towel to mop up the water. Of course, it was Barney who was suspicious. I was still holding him, all twenty-five pounds of him, when I stood up. He started to growl, a low, deep-throated sound like an old car left out in a winter storm. He was set to bark loud and long. I could hear heavy footsteps on the stairs. Automatically I put my hand over his mouth. In this situation a dog isn't protection; he's in danger. So I held his mouth shut tight. And then—*then*—I remembered the neighborhood burglaries. In two steps I was behind the high-backed chair. As I think back on that scene, I'm surprised no one drove by and wondered about a woman in jeans and kelly-green sweatshirt squatting down behind an armchair in front of the floor-to-ceiling windows. And holding twenty-five pounds of squirming fur. But no one must have passed by.

I held Barney tight, trying to pass on to him a calm I could barely fake. I peered out from behind the chair just long enough to see a tall, thin man all in white, even to the stocking over his head. He came up the stairs and turned to the left like he knew just what he was doing. As I said to the police later, it wouldn't be hard to case this "joint," what with windows on all sides. This guy had to have done so; burglars normally don't burgle in dress whites.

He was in the master bedroom for exactly seven minutes. I didn't move. He came out and walked right toward me. Barney's attempt at a growl had turned to a low moan. The burglar stopped. I didn't dare lift my head to see his reaction. I was sure he'd heard. But then the string section wailed over the sound system and I realized the burglar wasn't about to notice anything over Shostakovich. If he heard Barney at all, he must have assumed the moan was the wind. He turned toward the other bedroom—my room.

I held my breath. Now I could neither see nor hear him. The music was too loud. Why couldn't I have chosen Brahms? I expected as soon as the burglar spotted my clothes, he'd come looking for me. And in this white and glass house there was nowhere to hide. I was shaking. Barney was moaning away. The orchestra was blaring.

The burglar was in my room for nearly ten minutes. Now I know it must have taken him that long to get the safe open. By the time he came out, I was almost faint from fear. My legs had been quivering so violently, I'd dropped to the floor at minute number three and sat on my heels. At this point there was no way I could have run. He walked out of the bedroom with a pillowcase—white, of course— over his shoulder. You think bizarre things at a moment like that, and what struck me was that he looked like the ghost of Santa. I probably never should have let on to the police. But in any case, it was probably that thought that caused me to loosen my hand. Barney let out a howl, a huge frenzied bark, the bark of a dog who'd been waiting seventeen minutes to give the intruder what for. A bark that couldn't be mistaken for wind even if I'd been playing the 1812 Overture.

The burglar stopped dead.

Brave little Barney raced at him.

And—it still makes me furious when I think of it—the miserable brute kicked him! Poor little Barney went flying halfway across the room. It's just lucky he didn't hit the dining room table. Even so, he was shaking, and making an awful noise somewhere between a squeal and a growl. I raced over, and before I had him up in my arms, the door slammed and I realized the burglar had fled. It was only then that it struck me how lucky I was. And how outraged.

An engine started. I ran to the living room window in time to see a maroon pickup. A Dodge Ram truck with sides curved like a fist, a scratch along the passenger door, and license plate reading 2EXT1-something-something. Embroidery has given me a very good eye for detail.

I was still shaking as I called the police. But that calmed me, and as unnerving as the break-in had been, there was something about it not being my house that gave me a certain distance from the whole thing. When I put down the phone, I figured I'd barely have time to turn off the sound system so I wouldn't deafen the police, and, of course, to check out the condition of the two bedrooms.

In my room the closet door was wide open, as were the desk drawers and the safe. My things were untouched. It was almost insulting. But the master bedroom looked like the illustration for "tossed." Everything that would open was open. Dresser drawers were overturned, the shelves in the closet bared. The floor was covered in clothes, papers, and Melanie's costume jewelry. The good stuff, in fact the whole jewelry box, was gone.

As soon as the police walked in the atmosphere changed again. I no longer felt like the quizzical victim; I saw myself as a professional among professionals. Spotting the detective in charge, I strode up to him and made it clear. I said, "You may have been intent on capturing the burglar, but nowhere near as much as I am. I want that dog-kicker behind bars." And I have to say the way they assessed me seemed to change once I gave the vehicle description and license number. Of course they were sorry I didn't get the last two digits, but like I said to Detective Ambrose, "How many maroon Dodge Ram trucks can there be in the 2EXT 100s?"

He nodded, and that motion shifted his gaze lower. For a moment he was looking at my hand.

I glanced down too, moving only my eyes. I realized the awful possibility. Melanie Beckworth's sapphire ring sat right there on my finger. I was holding Barney and I don't think the detective saw much of the ring. Maybe just a hint of blue. Whatever, it was all I could do to hide my panic. I lowered my head, murmured to the dog, all the while trying to figure how to get out of there. I couldn't have the police asking how come a house sitter would have such an expensive ring. Maybe they don't ask that type of classist thing, but maybe means little when you're sitting in a cell. And once Melanie got home there'd be nothing so good as maybe. I had to move, and quick.

In my panic I must have given Barney a squeeze. He yelped. I said, "Detective, I've just got to get this poor little dog to the vet. I told you, didn't I, that the burglar kicked him? Poor little guy; he got it right in the ribs. He's only a little dog. He could have a cracked rib or internal damage, or . . ." As I went on I caressed Barney. I *had* felt around his side and I didn't think he was injured. (Despite the kick, I suspected with all the extra treats and attention he'd get from me, the vet, and Melanie when she got home, Barney probably would put this day in the plus column.) I suspect the detective thought the same, but he wasn't about to deny a taxpayer's dog medical attention. And the prospect of having every step of his investigation tailed by a crazed dog woman was probably more than he could stand.

Alas, he compromised. Instead of letting me put Barney in Melanie's car and head off, he had another cop drive me to the vet. He said it was a courtesy, but I couldn't help wondering it was so I wouldn't abscond with Melanie's car. The worst of it was that I could hardly take off the ring now. For the entire hour and forty-five minutes we sat in the vet's outer office, waiting to slip in between scheduled patients who were already backed up at this time of day, I couldn't move my hand from under the dog.

When I finally got back to Melanie's house, Detective Ambrose was sitting in his car looking like he'd been bitten.

"I was able to reach Mrs. Beckworth. She'll be back here in a couple hours. She said to send you on home."

I restrained a huge Whew! I hated to leave Barney alone, but I wasn't about to pass up the chance to get out of there before Melanie got home and spotted her ring. Still, the detective's creased brow and scrunched mouth worried me. With a cut-and-dried case like this he should be smiling. *Get out while you can,* common sense said. But I heard myself saying, "What's the matter?"

"Denny," he muttered.

"Denny?"

"The perp."

"You already know who the burglar is?" *Ambrose should have been smiling ear-to-ear!* And he definitely was not.

"We've got him in custody." *Thanks to you,* he might have added, but did not.

"So?"

"Nothing ties him to the crime. Nothing but your report. He swears he just stopped in the park. Swears he was never in the house."

"I suppose the bastard swears he never kicked the dog either! He probably swears—Detective, check his socks, his shoes, his pant legs. You're going to find dog hair."

Now Ambrose did smile, an expression that wavered between glee and embarrassment. But he was a professional and he'd probably been scooped before and not let that stand in his way. He got right back in his car and called the station. Then he insisted on waiting till I'd thrown my clothes in a suitcase and drove me home himself. Which meant I had to go through a whole new array of contortions to keep the damned ring out of sight.

But I did it, and when Ambrose left me off, he grinned and waved.

Rarely have I felt such relief getting back to my own little cell of an apartment. Still, it made me very uneasy that the burglar had been nabbed so fast. With each day that passed without a call from Ambrose, I was more relieved. But not relieved enough.

I don't think I slept for three nights straight. And twenty times a day I found myself thinking I should call Melanie and tell her I picked up her ring by mistake. But really, how could I? You don't ferret out and break into a woman's jewelry box *by mistake.*

On the fourth day, I spotted Ambrose downtown outside a Mexican take-out place. My first reaction was to cross the street and get away fast. But the suspense was killing me. I had to take a moment to think how an only-casually-interested person would behave. Forcing myself to slow down, I strolled toward him and was still pondering greetings when he noticed me. He smiled wide, strode right up to me and said, "Let me buy you lunch."

God forbid! "Thanks, but—"

"No, listen, it's the least I can do. If you hadn't told us about the dog hair, Denny'd've walked."

"That's great. But what about the stuff he stole?"

"Maybe it'll turn up at a pawnshop. Maybe. But I'll tell you, there's no sign of it. It could be on the other side of the country by now."

He said a few more things about trial and procedures, but I was barely listening because nothing was so important as the loot not being recovered. The jewelry box and its contents were gone. Never was Melanie Beckworth going to discover her sapphire ring—*my* sapphire ring—hadn't gone with it. I was so relieved I was tempted to reconsider lunch.

But I'm not a fool. And relieved as I was, I never

dreamed I would ever be able to wear that magnificent sapphire ring outside my own room.

But it's on my finger right now—I've had it sized down and it suits my third finger quite well. I do love seeing the sunlight glint off it.

And for this I have to thank Melanie. She gave me the ring.

Admittedly, she didn't do it as graciously as she might have.

Well, not graciously at all. In fact, she showed up at eight A.M. one morning the next week. She was pounding on my door. I barely got the chain off when she pushed inside. "You stole my ring!" she hissed.

"No, Melanie," I insisted, "you're wrong."

"Don't lie to me, I know you've got it. You have to have it!"

I put out my palm to stop her. My anxiety evaporated. I had heard all I needed. "Melanie, the reason I have your ring is that you gave it to me."

"I never—"

"Because I admired it and I'm such a good house sitter—"

"Why would I—"

"No, Melanie, not why, but how. Your whole jewelry box was stolen. How would you know I had one ring that should have been in it?" I patted her arm. "Of course you're upset. And it's easy to forget a small gift when you have so much on your mind. But don't give me another thought. You've got enough on your mind with your accomplice in jail."

I was tempted to insist that she give me Barney too. But like I said, I don't like to presume.

Oklahoma resident Carolyn Hart, author of two different series, one featuring bookseller Annie Darling and the other former journalist Henrie O, has won Agatha Awards for Best Novel for Something Wicked *and* Dead Man's Island. *Her most recent novels include the Agatha-nominated* Death on the River Walk *and* Sugarplum Dead. *This story highlights the vengeance of a woman scorned—and a number of sudden turns . . .*

Turnaround

Carolyn Hart

Damn. She'd forgotten the tickets! Leigh Graham Porter swerved her silver Jag into the alley that ran behind the houses. She parked by the stone wall next to the gate. She'd slip quietly up to the house and get them without Brian knowing. It would be so much more fun tonight to hand the tickets to Brian. He would open the folder, lift them out, two tickets to Tahiti, and then his lips would curve into that lazy, crooked, sensuous smile. That moment would cap a romantic evening at The Ivy, the wonderful restaurant where he'd proposed to her four years ago today.

Leigh was smiling as she walked through the gate of the bougainvillea-draped wall. All right, she was proud to have Brian Winslow—tall, blond, athletic, thirtyish Brian—as her third husband. Whenever she saw her first husband at parties, he with his much younger trophy wife, dark-eyed seductive Courtney, Leigh and Hal exchanged cordial smiles of mutual understanding.

Youth was all that mattered in Hollywood, but she and Hal were still surviving. Leigh's body was Jane Fonda hard. No one would ever guess that she was past fifty, her black hair lustrous, her face smooth, her wide-set green eyes glowing with health and success. She continued to sell screenplays for enough money to afford Brian and a turreted house in Beverly Hills and a sprawling Palm Springs hacienda. To remember the long ago lean years, she'd kept her first little house in Topanga Canyon, and it was still a favorite retreat, especially to spend moonlit nights there with Brian. She walked a little faster, tendrils of vine brushing against her designer jeans. Perhaps she'd call in sick, skip the script meeting, stay home with Brian this morning. She was almost to the terrace when she heard his voice. She smiled indulgently. He always carried the portable phone outside with him and stretched out in the hammock to make calls. Yes, he was a creature who loved all comforts. But so was she.

". . . you shouldn't call here. I know. Yes, she's gone, but what if she ran late? Let's not take any chances now, Holly. We're so close . . ."

Leigh stopped behind the hibiscus. Brian was on the other side. He could not be more than a few feet away, his deep voice achingly familiar, and that softness when he said—

"I love you, too. Of course I do. Trust me, it's going to work out . . . No, there's no chance of failure. It's all set. Then I'll be free."

Leigh crossed her arms against her body, struggled to breathe.

"Don't worry. Thursday night at the Topanga Canyon house. She thinks I'm meeting her there." He spoke briskly. He might have been describing a train connection.

Leigh felt the warm track of tears down her cheeks.

"You don't need to know about that, Holly. I've got a deal with a friend. One shot and it's over. I've got it all figured out. I'll have an alibi that can't be broken. A car wreck. She's going to get to the house about seven-thirty. When she arrives, the door will be open. She'll think I'm already there and walk in and that will be that. Then we'll be together forever. God, I love you . . ."

Leigh edged softly away from the terrace, her goal the kitchen door. Brian never came into the kitchen. Rosa wouldn't be there yet; she didn't come to work until ten. Leigh reached the door, stepped inside. She took off her shoes, held them in her hand, ran up the back stairs in her stocking feet. When she reached her office, she hurried to her desk, looked down at the blinking Caller ID: Holly Fraser and a Valley number. She reached for a pen, repeating the number over and over in her mind. The light blinked off and the name and number disappeared as Brian deleted the listing.

In only a moment Brian's Porsche—the Porsche she'd bought him for his birthday—roared down the drive to the street. Leigh's face was hard. She knew Brian loved that car. He must really be willing to make a sacrifice to wreck his Porsche.

Her eyes traveled to her desk calendar. Today was Tuesday. According to Brian, she had two days to live.

She began to pace, the way she always worked, waiting for fragments of thoughts to swirl into a pattern. They always did for her. Critics lauded the brilliance of her plots. Thursday night . . . the canyon house . . . a hired killer . . . but what if . . .

Leigh was aware of admiring glances from men at nearby tables and the icy jealousy of their women. She knew she looked especially lovely, her dark hair in a soft French roll, the kind that teased a man to loosen it and let it fall, her hard body alluring beneath the silver sheath dress. She sparkled like a many faceted diamond. Brian, of course, puffed with satisfaction, smugly certain that her uncommon iridescence grew out of passion for him.

He flipped open the ticket folder. "Tahiti! Leigh, you're unbelievable."

Was there a tinge of regret in his deep voice? Why hadn't he asked for a divorce? But Leigh knew the answer to that. She'd never been a fool, and the prenuptial agreement accorded him nothing if there was a divorce. Brian would be a very rich widower.

Leigh's lips curved in a merry smile. She picked up her champagne glass. "Brian, I have something even more special for you." Her exhilaration came not from champagne, but from the intoxication of danger.

He quirked a blond brow, leaned forward, his eyes full of warmth.

Her smile never wavered. "I've written a script that will be perfect for you—"

His eyes widened and his mouth parted. She'd let him read lines in her scripts, but she'd never made an effort to help him audition. Why should she? Why expose him to the temptations of hungry young actresses willing to barter body and soul for any perceived advantage. And a recommendation to be in a Leigh Graham Porter film was to die for.

"—and tomorrow morning I'll make a video and take it to Cameron Bachman with the script."

Cameron Bachman was currently the most successful movie director in the business.

Leigh held out the fluted glass. "To us. Forever."

Brian hesitated for only an instant, then his glass clicked against hers. He didn't repeat the toast.

The videocam was set up beside the desk. Leigh leaned against the desk. "Here's the story. You're in love with this girl. You've loved her forever. But you quarreled. She ran away and married a bandleader. He's abusive. You hear about her problems, how she's shown up at her sister's house with a bruised face, even been to the E.R. Anyway," Leigh waved her hand, "you've gotten in touch with her, she knows you care. You'd planned to meet her at your sister's house just before dark. Your sister gets called out of town. The girl's scared to be alone with you in case her husband finds out. So," Leigh pulled loose a sheet of script, "here's your sides. Let's see what you can do." Her voice was crisp now, businesslike, professional. "I'll do the voice-over." She slipped on her tortoiseshell-rimmed glasses and picked up the script. Not, of course, a script that she'd written on her computer. It was an easy matter to drive to Pasadena, find a Kinko's that rented use of computers. She'd worn a red wig, baggy gray sweats, and paid cash. She reached out, adjusted the angle of the camera, turned it on, then casually leaned back against the desk, one hand behind her to flip on the tape recorder. One finger rested lightly on the Stop key. "Okay, Brian. Lots of emotion. Let's go."

EXT. CITY STREET—NIGHT

To establish—

EXT. PHONE BOOTH—NIGHT

Jarvis runs to booth, quickly punches out number, looks over his shoulder as if fearful.

> JARVIS
>
> It's me. Listen, plans have changed. She's going out of town. Meet me there, seven-thirty.

> EILEEN   *(v.o., filtered)*
>
> I can't. He'll . . .

> JARVIS
>
> We'll have a wonderful night, just you and me. And next week, we'll be together.

> EILEEN   *(v.o., filtered)*
>
> I—I want to be with you—

> JARVIS
>
> I love you. Don't disappoint me. I've got to go. Don't call me. Someone's . . .

She took two takes, then clapped her hands. "Brian, you are so *good*. Cameron will be blown away. I'll take the script and videotape to his office this afternoon."

Thursday morning Leigh's eyes glowed like a cat's as Brian walked to the garage with her. As she slipped behind the wheel, he tangled a finger in her dark hair. "Hell, I wish you didn't have to go to the damn production meeting."

Leigh smiled up at him, touched his cheek with her finger, drew it down slowly to his lips. "I could call in, say I was sick."

His eyes flared just for an instant. His laugh was hearty. "Not you, Leigh. You don't want them making decisions about your script without you there."

"As if I'd have any choice," she said dryly.

"Besides," his tone was rueful, "the guys'll kill me if I don't show up to play."

"Oh, yes, today's your regular game." Yes, she remembered that well. Every Thursday morning, Brian played doubles at the Beverly Hills Country Club. "And you're right. I can't miss this meeting." She smiled at him. "How well you know me." Yes, she was a fighter. Often if a studio bought a screenplay then changed its mind and the script went into turnaround, she used every contact she had to find the screenplay a new home. Soon he would know just how hard she was willing to fight for whatever belonged to her, including her life. "All day I'll be thinking about tonight. I'll see you at the canyon house."

She parked in the alley, waited until it was past time for Brian's tennis to start. In her office, she carried the tape player and the portable phone to a window overlooking the drive. She'd hear the Porsche if he returned early. She was taking no chances. Her lips moved in a cold smile. Brian thought he wasn't taking any chances. Ah, to be young and to live and learn.

She punched in the numbers.

A breathless voice, a sweet young voice, answered. "Hello."

Leigh pushed the button and the carefully edited tape ran:

"It's me. Listen, plans have changed. She's going out of town. Meet me there, seven-thirty. We'll have a wonderful night, just you and me. And next week we'll be together. I love you. Don't disappointment me. I've got to go. Don't call me. Someone's . . ."

"Brian, what—"

Leigh clicked off the phone.

Leigh took her time in the office. She found the sides, tucked one into her purse, tore the rest into shreds, flushed them down the toilet.

Leigh left the production meeting early, drove back to Beverly Hills. Brian wouldn't leave the house until after seven. He'd time the car wreck for around seven-fifteen. There would be a wait for the cops to come. But later, no one could ever suggest he'd been in Topanga Canyon. As alibis went, it was clever.

Leigh turned the Jag into their drive shortly after seven. She left the car running. The Jag was blocking the drive, but that wouldn't occur to Brian. She ran up the front steps, unlocked the door, flung it open, shouting, "Brian, Brian!"

He was coming down the stairs. He stopped and stared at her, his handsome face slack with shock.

"Brian, I've got the most wonderful news. I had a call from Cameron. He caught me just before I was leaving for the canyon. But that doesn't matter. You know how he is." She threw up both hands in exasperation. "He always has to do things at once. And his way. He'll audition you tonight. At his house. This may be your chance!"

She turned south on the San Diego freeway. Traffic was heavy. Finally, she reached 5 South, but rush hour traffic stalled them for more than an hour. "He lives to hell and gone." Her tone was irritated. "But he gave me directions. He's back in the hills down near Laguna. You concentrate on your lines."

Brian practiced.

Leigh listened in rapt admiration. Occasionally, she

made a suggestion. She drove as dusk turned to darkness. She turned off the 5, took a road into the hills, a twisting, hairpin road that skirted canyons. It was almost ten when she finally gave up. She stopped at the side of the road, got out her cell phone, scrabbled through her purse. "Damn, I thought I had his number. And it's unlisted. Oh Brian, I'm so sorry. I'll call first thing in the morning. I have his number in my Rolodex. Cameron's a good guy. He'll understand." A trill of laughter. "He knows I have the world's lousiest sense of direction."

Brian didn't laugh.

Leigh held the muscle relaxant tablets in her hand. One or two? One should be enough. Be damned awkward if there were an overdose. Using the back of a spoon, she ground the pill into white powder, scraped the powder into a wineglass. She poured in champagne, stirred, carefully set that glass at the front of the tray on the left side. She didn't fill the second glass quite so full.

She waited a few minutes, then carried the tray upstairs and knocked on Brian's door. She opened it.

Brian swung around, his face tight with irritation. He wouldn't keep those boyish good looks frowning like that. She noted his blue silk pajamas. Yes, she'd given him time to change. He'd tossed his gray slacks onto the sofa. "Brian"—Leigh stretched out his name like a dramatic festival tattoo—"I brought champagne to celebrate. Tomorrow will be the most unforgettable day of your life."

She handed him the glass on the left, picked up the nearby glass, raised it high. "To tomorrow and the new life of Brian Winslow."

The glasses clicked with a light chime. They drank.

In her room, Leigh changed unhurriedly from her silk tee and beige jeans into a long-sleeve black turtleneck, black jeans, black sneakers. She tucked money and a driver's license into her pocket. It took a moment to find a pair of gloves, since neither the society nor the climate required them. But there were soft doeskin driving gloves tucked in a winter coat she'd bought for location shooting in New York. She glanced at the clock. Just past midnight.

Brian's door was closed. She didn't bother to knock. She opened the door. He was sprawled on his back across the foot of his bed, mouth wide, breathing stertorous. She moved quickly, snatched up his slacks with her gloved hands. "Sweet dreams, little man." She checked the pockets, a tight frown thinning her mouth. Where was the sides he'd practiced? Not in the pockets. She glanced around the room, saw the sheet lying on the bedside stand. She grabbed it up, carried it to the bathroom, ripped the page into tiny pieces, flushed them away.

Leigh drove past the turnoff to the cliff road twice. On her third pass, reassured by the silence and the dark, she turned onto the narrow, rutted, twisting road. Always before, the rustic, almost hidden entrance had appealed, the gateway to privacy and adventure. Now her heart thudded uncomfortably. Once on the road, she was trapped by anyone coming in after her. No one should come, of course. She'd considered parking along the road and walking up. But it was almost a mile to the house, and someone might see the parked car, note the license plate. If all went well, she could be up and down the road in a quarter hour at the most.

Leigh drove without lights, easing the car up the twisting road, using the moonlight as her guide. At the top of the grade she paused, studying the dark house. No lights, no movement. She turned into the drive, carefully turned and backed until the car was facing downhill. If she had to hurry . . .

She turned off the motor, listened to the swish of the pines and the crash of the waves far below. Her hands gripped the steering wheel. She should move now, this instant, hurry from the car, run across the graveled drive, up the steps to the redwood deck. Still she sat.

An owl hooted. What was that crackling sound? She jerked her head so quickly her neck hurt. Her heart thudded. Oh, God. She could scarcely hear above the roar in her ears. Slowly she sorted out the sounds, the crash of the waves, the sough of tree limbs, the rustle of shrubbery.

Leigh held tight to the wheel. She wanted desperately to turn on the motor and careen down the canyon, away from this pocket of dark and quiet, this isolated house and the malevolence that seemed so near. But she had no choice. There was no turning back.

She opened the door, slipped out of the car, leaving the door a little ajar. She forced herself to walk quickly. The faster she moved, the sooner she could be out of here. She carried Brian's trousers in one hand, a small pocket flashlight in the other. She didn't need the flashlight. Moonlight bathed the deck, turning the dark windows to patches of silver.

The front door stood open. That's what Brian had planned, the open door and she stepping inside. One step, another, Leigh moved like a shadow across the deck. She eased open the screen door, stepped into the living room. She flicked on the flashlight and stared across the shining expanse of wood—she'd always been pleased with the white pine floors, such a dramatic contrast to the red cypress of the walls—at the body sprawled only a few feet away. The blood spatters were stark and ugly against the shell-pink dress and white wood floor. The young woman lay on her back, thrown there by the force of the shot.

Blond hair curved against a lace-white cheek. Dead green eyes stared emptily into eternity.

Leigh shuddered. She struggled to breathe, heard her own voice, high and stricken, "No, no, no . . ." She'd not realized how terrible this would be. She flung out her arms, the light of the flash dancing crazily around the dark room. Brian's trousers slapped against the door frame. She looked at the gray worsted slacks, then turned her head toward the murdered woman. Her hand steadied, light spilling over the still form.

That could be her body. That would be her body if she hadn't overheard Brian's clever plan. This woman had known. This woman had been willing for her to die. She owed her nothing.

Hands shaking, the trousers dangling in front of her, Leigh walked toward the body. Averting her eyes from the dead white face, she leaned forward, swiped the pants against that bloodied chest.

A click.

She froze. What was that sound? She jerked the flashlight around the room. Nothing moved. The dark shadows behind the furniture might harbor a thousand screaming devils of her imagination, but there was no one in this room except her and the forever still body.

All right, all right. God, how long had she been here? Too long. Time to move now. Fast. She hurried across the room to the wet bar, stepped behind, stuffed the trousers beneath the sink.

She didn't glance again toward the body. Everything was done now. Let Brian reap what he had sown. She clattered across the deck and down the stairs, ran to the car.

Three weeks later Leigh carried the *Times* to her favorite chair by the pool.

SCREENWRITER'S HUSBAND
CHARGED IN CABIN DEATH

Brian Winslow, husband of Oscar-winning screenwriter Leigh Graham Porter, was charged with first-degree murder today in the shooting death April 4 of Holly Fraser, a young actress he met while filming an unsuccessful TV pilot two years ago.

Winslow's attorney entered a plea of Not Guilty. Winslow is accused of shooting Fraser, 26, at the Topanga Canyon home owned by his wife. No motive has been established, and police said Winslow and Fraser had remained friends after the filming.

Winslow claims he spent the evening of the murder in the company of his wife. Porter has not responded to interview requests. However, intimates of the writer have said that Porter was shocked by her husband's statement. According to friends, Porter was home alone that evening and didn't see her husband. Further, Porter expressed surprise at his story of an audition for one of her scripts. She told a friend that she'd never written a script suitable for her husband. Porter is reported to have said that she didn't believe Winslow would shoot anyone. However, Winslow remains jailed, as he has been unable to post the $100,000 bail and Porter has declined to post bail.

Although police have not released details of their investigation, there is reason to believe . . .

Leigh dropped the paper on the wicker table, picked up her espresso, and reached for a script on the glass-topped table. The harder she worked, the easier it was to push away the memory of those dead green eyes.

The plain manila envelope was tucked into the mailbox when Leigh returned from the studio the next evening. She frowned as she picked it up. It was too light to be a script. It was amazing how often hopeful writers cornered her at cocktail parties, tucked scripts into the mailbox. What a bore. But this envelope couldn't hold much. Her name was written in a flowing script. That was all.

She carried the envelope into the kitchen, sniffed. Hmm. Rosa was such a good cook. What would it be this evening? She glanced at the note on the kitchen block. Dove casserole and rice. She poured a glass of Chablis, almost tossed the envelope into the wastebasket, shrugged, opened it.

A photograph dropped onto the pale yellow tiles of the cooking island.

Leigh's eyes widened. Her breath stopped. A hard pressure filled her chest. The wineglass slipped from her fingers, shattering on the red tile floor. Leigh stared at the picture, the telling, damning, hideous picture: the dark walls, the white floor, the dead girl, her open eyes, the blood that had welled across her pink dress, and Leigh leaning down, swiping Brian's gray trousers against the body. The flashlight pointed down toward the body, but Leigh's face was clear and distinct, her eyes hard, cheekbones jutting, lips pressed into a thin line.

Nausea welled in Leigh's throat. A wave of heat swept her. She crumpled the slick eight by ten photograph and shuddered. She'd thought herself alone with death, but she had not been alone. Someone watched, watched and waited, and when the moment was perfect, held the camera rock steady and pressed the button. There'd been no flash. But there need not have been, not with high speed film and the right lens aperture.

Fear washed over her. Where had this film been developed? Who had seen it? But there had likely been a casual explanation of publicity stills for a local playhouse. Who would ever question any kind of pose in this town? No doubt the film was taken to a one-hour photo shop and a false name given, the prints paid for with cash. Who would remember after time passed?

The negative.

A pulse quivered in Leigh's throat. The negative didn't matter. Any number of copies could be made from a photograph now. So, no matter how much she paid, there could always be copies in reserve.

Paid.

That was the point of this photograph, wasn't it?

Whirling, she grabbed the envelope, the unmarked plain manila envelope, ripped it open. Nothing. The envelope was empty. Reluctantly, she spread out the crumpled photograph, turned it over. Nothing on the back. In a frenzy, she ripped the photo into tiny pieces, carried them to the sink, hunted for matches. There had to be some matches somewhere—

The phone rang.

Leigh stared at the bright lemon portable phone.

Another peal. Another.

Stiffly, she reached out, picked up the receiver, pushed the button. She held the phone to her ear. She didn't speak. She knew who was calling, who had to be calling. It didn't matter when the envelope was delivered. The photographer—no, be plain, be honest, she told herself—the murderer, the friend Brian had asked to murder her, had only to park down the street, waiting until her silver Jag turned into the drive, allowing her time enough to find the envelope, open it, see the hellish picture.

The whisper was slow in coming. "Photography is an art, isn't it, Leigh?"

She stared at the Caller ID bar: *Unavailable.*

"Don't you like my picture?" The whisper was sexless, ageless, a wisp of sound.

Her throat was so dry, it hurt to talk. She pushed out the words, dropped them like steel balls into a cavern. "What do you want?"

"You get right to the point, I see. Very well. But I'll give you time to think about the future. Oh, say, until tomorrow. There's a pay phone at the Rite-Aid on Canon not far from your house. Be there at ten o'clock in the morning."

Leigh stared at her reflection in the shiny plate glass of the Rite-Aid. She looked old, her eyes bloodshot, her face pasty. She'd lain wakeful most of the night. When fatigue pulled her into sleep, she'd jerked awake at every sound, and in her mind a photograph expanded, grew larger and larger, until all she could see was dead staring eyes. She leaned against the plastic side of the pay phone, smelled that essentially California mixture of car fumes, gasoline, and eucalyptus, and waited.

How much money would he want? What else could she do but pay up? If she told the truth to the police, she was an accomplice to murder. A lizard slithered along the rock wall by the hedge. Accomplice? More than that. Though it seemed only fair. But the police didn't care about fair.

The phone rang. Leigh yanked up the receiver.

The whisper was as insubstantial as fog, but the words permeated her soul. "You're guilty of murder."

"No." The denial burst from her. "You were going to kill me. You were going to kill me!"

"You could have called the police."

Leigh felt her body shrink and tighten. That's what everyone would say.

"But you didn't." The whisper was silky. "Somehow you found out what was planned. I was waiting. I heard the footsteps running across the deck. As soon as she stepped inside, I shot. As you'll discover, it isn't easy to do. I wanted to get it over with. If I'd waited a minute, seen her better . . . But I didn't. Of course, after I shot, I had to be sure you were dead. Imagine my surprise—"

"Stop it." Leigh's voice rose. "Stop whispering!"

"Oh, I don't have much more to say." The whisper was even lighter, fainter. "The minute I saw the dead girl, I knew what had happened. I knew who she was, but it was too late. Too late for her and for Brian. But not too late for me. I knew you must have arranged for her to come. But I knew you wouldn't stop there."

Leigh's fingers tightened around the sticky receiver.

"I was sure you'd implicate Brian. That meant putting some kind of physical evidence in the house. I took a chance and went to get a camera."

Thoughts whipped in her mind: . . . left and came back . . . how far could he live . . . he could have stopped, bought one . . . no way of knowing . . .

"How much do you want?" She tried to keep her voice even, but it cracked as she spoke. She was afraid, so damn afraid.

A husky laugh. "I don't want money, Leigh."

A car squealed out of the parking lot, the fumes choking her. Leigh didn't move. She stared at the black metal box.

"Brian and I had a deal. No one would ever suspect me of shooting you, and no one would ever suspect him of shooting a man quite unknown to him. I was to shoot his bete noir, he was to shoot mine. He was to have an un-breakable alibi at the time of your death. I will have an un-breakable alibi this coming Saturday night."

"You're out of your mind." She began to shake. She had a sudden sharp clear memory of Robert Walker and Farley Granger in the classic *Strangers on a Train*. But this was so much worse. She'd never planned anyone's death. She pushed away the picture of the girl's dead green eyes. That hadn't been her plan. Holly died because of Brian and this nameless creature with the hideous whisper.

Soft laughter. "Aren't we all for living in La-La Land? But it's quid pro quo, Leigh. You'll do quite as well as Brian. Now," the whisper was brisk, "when you get home, go down to the alley. There's a backpack inside your gate. You'll find detailed instructions in it. Who you are going to kill and when."

"I can't." Leigh's chest squeezed.

"You can. You will." The whisper was cold and determined. "A final note, Leigh, don't try to be clever. You can't find me. There are too many people who want this man dead. His wife. His son. His daughter. His ex-mistress. His business partner. And I've made it easy for you. You'll find the gun in the backpack. Zero hour? Saturday night, Leigh, nine o'clock."

The connection broke.

Leigh gripped the receiver. She struggled to breathe. Pay phone. The killer sent her here so she couldn't see the number on Caller ID . . .

Leigh scrabbled in her purse, her fingers desperately seeking coins. She found one, two, jammed them into slots, punched *69. There was a pause, a squeal, a recorded voice, "Call return service is not . . ."

Oh damn, damn, damn.

Leigh stared at the blue nylon backpack lying in deep shade next to the oleander. It held death. She didn't want to touch it, not ever. But she had to . . . She wore gardening gloves, carried the pack at arm's length into the garage to a worktable. She unbuckled the plastic snaps, pulled out a manila envelope. She left the gun in the dark interior. It was hard to open the envelope with her clumsily gloved hands. A studio portrait slipped to the cement floor. Leigh creased the picture as she picked it up.

Sunlight spilled through the window above the work-bench. She studied the face. An Alan Alda type, but tougher, harder, with a sensuous mouth and combative eyes. Across the bottom, scrawled in a bold masculine script, was the inscription and name, *Love, Jake.*

She pulled two sheets of paper, both computer gener-ated, from the envelope and a driver's license with her pho-tograph. The name on the license was Ellen Vorhees and the address was in Long Beach. On one sheet was a map of an elegant backyard with a legend identifying sites, with a star by the Fortune Teller booth near the swimming pool. The second sheet contained instructions.

Leigh read swiftly, picking out the important facts. Sat-urday night the county bar association was having a fund-raising carnival at a house three streets from her home. Jake Garrison was volunteering as a swami in the fortune-telling booth from eight-thirty to nine-thirty.

And:

> *The back flap of the tent will be unfastened. At nine o'clock, pull aside the flap, shoot Jake, drop the gun, meld into the crowd. You may be able to slip away down the alley. If not, the police will take names and IDs. You'll have one. But no one will ever find Ellen Vorhees. You will receive the photograph you desire in the next mail. Good hunting.*

Jake Garrison. Attorney at law. Personal injury lawyer specializing in medical malpractice. Facts welled from his law firm's website, so many that Leigh didn't try to absorb them all. She found everything she needed to know about his wife, Ingrid; his son, Bobby; his daughter, Tina; his partner, Ray Porter. She found their ages, histories. And phone numbers.

Leigh tilted back her chair and stared at the screen. If she were the Whisperer, she wouldn't have included herself among the suggested villains.

Who hates medical malpractice lawyers?

Leigh shot a glance at the clock. She'd been at her computer ever since she got home from the pay phone, almost four hours. Her eyes ached, her head throbbed. The time, so little time, how could she find out in time . . . All right, all right. She had to narrow the search, set up parameters. She could rule out lawsuits against hospitals and HMOs. It had to be personal. Someone who had been damaged, perhaps irrevocably, by Garrison. Or, better yet, someone close to trial who might believe his death could make a difference. Yes, that was the route to take.

Leigh ended up with four names: a doctor who operated while high on drugs, a doctor who amputated the wrong leg, a doctor who misdiagnosed ovarian cancer, and a doctor whose liposuction patient died. Four names . . . Leigh rubbed her aching head and stared at the list. Abruptly, she jolted back her chair, ran down the hall to Brian's room. She grabbed the doorknob, flung the door open, hurried to the bath. Flicking on the light, she crossed to the medicine cabinet, opened it. She reached up, grabbed a handful of plastic vials.

Oh shit, yes. There it was. A painkiller after his knee surgery. Prescribed by Dr. Annabelle Smith. The same Dr. Annabelle Smith who had amputated a left leg instead of a right. Yes, yes, yes! Hello, Whisperer.

Leigh called Dr. Smith's home number at shortly after five. Voice mail picked up. Leigh didn't identify herself. If she'd found the Whisperer, no identification was needed. "Hello, Annabelle. I've been giving some thought to our conversation earlier today. I haven't yet informed Jake Garrison. I won't unless we can't make a deal. I suggest we get together at ten o'clock tonight at my house. You bring the picture and film. I'll have the backpack. Fair exchange. We both walk away with no hard feelings. See you then."

Ten o'clock came and went, of course. Leigh didn't expect Dr. Smith to respond to her summons. Not at the stated time. But she felt certain Dr. Smith would come very late, long after the appointed hour, when she should be deep in sleep. And easy to kill.

The house was dark and quiet. The only light came from security lights in the trees. It was just before three o'clock in the morning. Leigh waited in the deep shadow at the end of the patio, curled in a dark wicker chair. She had a good view of the back gate and the side yard. Her hair was tucked beneath a navy ball cap. She wore a black sweater, jeans, dark sneakers. She sipped a cup of strong black coffee, not that she was likely to drift into sleep. She felt oddly calm and perhaps a little exhilarated. This afternoon she'd been in a deadly box. Now she had a chance. If Dr. Smith was the Whisperer . . . Leigh shook her head impatiently. It couldn't be a coincidence, the doctor's trial set to begin next month and her name on Brian's medicine bottle. Dr. Smith was the Whisperer, smart, cunning, careful, dangerous, and a gambler. The Whisperer would come tonight, prepared to kill. Leigh sipped her coffee and waited, the gun heavy on her lap. Occasionally, she reached down to touch the heavy twine she'd tied to the switch that would turn on the patio lights.

The gate creaked. The squeal had to be unnerving to the doctor. Metal hinges scraped. A dark figure moved cautiously on the path, a small carryall in one hand.

Leigh watched, part of her mind at a distant remove, admiring the grace and stealth of the approach, part of her mind boring toward the moment when the lights would come on. Not yet. Not yet. Wait until the intruder was at a disadvantage. Leigh's hand gripped the twine. Wait, wait . . .

Enough light spilled down from the trees to illuminate the intruder's dark cap, black sweater, saggy black cardigan, shiny vinyl gloves, skintight black bike pants. No wonder she hadn't heard a car. Annabelle—surely they were on a first name basis now—had probably parked nearby. Her car must have a bike rack.

Annabelle stopped at the base of a tree with a limb that stretched over the second-story sun porch. She opened the carryall, pulled out a rope ladder. Dropping the small bag, she took a step nearer the tree, flung the ladder up. It took two tries before the hooks caught.

Leigh's hand tightened on the twine, yanked. Light blazed on the patio.

Annabelle froze on the rope ladder, halfway to the limb.

"Stay there." Leigh's voice was as sharp and hard as the click of a safety catch. She held the gun in both hands, aimed it.

Annabelle hung on the ladder, twisting to look down. The cap made her broad face look heavy. Burning dark eyes that slitted into fury. The long thin mouth quivered.

"Come down slowly. Yes, that's right. Put your hands up." Leigh was poised to shoot. She didn't want to. Not here. But if she had to . . .

The vinyl-gloved hands lifted, shiny in the lights of the patio. The hands of a killer.

Leigh watched those deep-socketed, furious eyes. "Don't move." The carryall—a blue canvas gym bag—lay near Annabelle's feet. "Shove the bag with your foot."

Cautiously, Leigh eased close enough to snag the bag

with her foot. She felt the hardness of a gun, gave a quick glance, felt the tightness ease out of her shoulders. Triumph almost made her giddy. She was in charge now. She had the only weapon. Now to get Annabelle into the garage . . . Her mind shied away from the next moment. But she had no choice. A quick shot. She'd already spread big black garbage sacks on the cement floor. The rest would be hard, getting the body into the trunk, driving to a remote area of the San Gabriel Mountains, dumping the grisly load. There was a road near the Mount Wilson Observatory . . . There would be no connection between her and a body found there.

"Walk up to the garage. I'm right behind you." And in a hurry, a big hurry.

Annabelle slowly moved ahead of her. "I'll make a deal. I've got the picture—and the negative—in my car."

"Too little too late, Annabelle." They were at the side door to the garage. "Open the door." Leigh's hands tightened on the gun.

Annabelle grabbed the knob and pulled. "It's stuck."

Leigh prodded her with the gun. They were almost there, almost inside the garage. Impatiently, she pressed nearer. "Turn it—" Leigh never finished.

Annabelle's right hand plunged into her cardigan pocket and out and up.

Leigh glimpsed the needle, felt a sharp, hot prick in her neck. In her last moment of life, Leigh squeezed the gun, heard the shots, knew that Annabelle fell as she herself sagged into oblivion.

Melodie Johnson Howe began her career as an actress and appeared in films with Mickey Rooney and Clint Eastwood before she turned to mystery writing and teaching. An Agatha nominee for Best First Novel for The Mother Shadow, *Howe followed up this book with* Beauty Dies. *Howe draws on her film background for this story featuring an aging actress and a best-selling author with less than charitable thoughts on their minds . . .*

Acting Tips

Melodie Johnson Howe

"Aren't you Nora Gray?" Meg West asked me in her harsh intrusive voice.

I'd been trying to get her to notice me for the last two days, ever since I put myself into this damn sanitarium. I was sitting on the verandah, my hair defiantly blond, no sunglasses, and wearing my silver mink coat. Hardly incognito for a great actress. But Meg walked around in her own world, where reality, and I might add truth, were of no consequence. *Writers!*

She squinted myopically into my face. "My God, you *are* Nora Gray!"

I nodded, smiling benignly as if she were just any fan.

"Do you know who I am?" she asked suspiciously.

"No."

(*Acting Tip: Much can be done with the tiny word "no." Most actresses let the little negative drop from their lips like a small rock onto cement, creating a thud. I let it float from my mouth like a bubble, so the receiver of this word can study it from all angles until it pops and disappears, leaving a haunting sense of rejection. To get this effect you must learn to control your breathing. The same can be done with the word "yes." Though I prefer to hiss this word like a snake. To do this you must let your breath slowly slide out through your clenched teeth. But for my needs, to answer "Yes" would not have the lie shimmering behind it.*)

"Should I know you?" I offered her my profile, still strong after all these years.

"Cut the crap. You're following me."

"Following you? I'm sorry but—"

"I don't know how you got in here, but you leave me alone, do you understand?"

"I'm afraid that you entered *my* space, as they say nowadays. I did not enter *yours*. Are you feeling all right? Would you like me to get you an attendant?" She did look frail.

"If I were all right I wouldn't be in here. Stay away from me!" She stalked off.

Smiling, I leaned back in my chair and turned my face to the sun, waiting for Meg to return; I knew her writer's curiosity would draw her back to me.

I had found out that Meg West was in the Silver Shadows Sanitarium through an old gossip columnist friend of mine. I had no trouble putting myself into this place. The doctors of Silver Shadows love to take in famous people who have cracked; the famous, especially when desperate, are always good for business.

(*Acting Tip: When performing a nervous breakdown, do not go over the top by sobbing and throwing yourself around the set; this will make you and your audience dizzy, and drive the cameraman into a real nervous breakdown. Pick an action that is out of the norm for your character. For example, I started wearing an old silver mink coat I had bought in the late fifties. Nobody could convince me to take it off. The sanitarium welcomed me with open arms.*)

Still leaning back in my chair, with my trademark violet-colored eyes closed against the sun, I slipped my right hand into my pocket and through the hole I had cut there a week earlier. Reaching my fingers down between the silky lining and the rough dried skin of the pelts, I found the gun I had placed in my coat's hem. I carefully pulled it up and into my pocket, letting the little weapon rest in my hand.

"Let's get this over with." Meg's voice cut sharply through my heart.

"I beg your pardon?" I slowly opened my eyes and blinked at her.

"Let's stop the playacting and talk girl-to-girl."

"Since I'm sixty-eight, and you're no spring chicken, I prefer woman-to-woman."

"Nora Gray admitting her age?" She painfully eased her very thin frame into the wicker chair next to mine.

"I've never understood," I chatted, "why women lie about their age. There are so many more important things to lie about. Now, just who are you?"

Placing her pointy elbow firmly on the chair's arm, she rested her sharp-as-a-knife chin in her hand. With her graying hair cut short she looked just like her photograph on the back of her book.

"You know who I am. Meg West. Critic-slash-author."

The important word to remember here is slash.

"Meg West!" I exclaimed.

(*Acting Tip: When looking surprised or shocked, don't—I repeat, don't—let your eyes go wide and your mouth fall open. This is not only unattractive, but it's also a ludicrous reaction. Keep your lips pressed together and your eyes focused on that which is shocking you; this will bring a natural tension to your face. If the script is good, the audience will fill in the proper array of emotions. If the script is trash, take the money and run.*)

"I can't believe it; so you're Meg West."

"As if you didn't know. I received every one of your poisonous, hateful letters."

"But how should I know you? We've never met in person." I rubbed my fingers along the inlaid ivory of the gun; I admit to buying the prettiest one. "I hope my letters didn't put you in Silver Shadows?" I asked, thoughtfully.

"Don't flatter yourself."

"Then maybe the burden of being a woman who knows everything was a little too much for you?"

"The book I wrote about you was a study; a *do's* and *dont's* on growing old. I knew if I used a famous woman, then ordinary women would read my book and be helped. And they were. I got thousands of letters thanking me."

"If you wrote about an ordinary woman, no one would have read it."

"Ordinary women come up to me on the street and tell me how I have given them the courage to age, to grow old. They thank me for making them understand they don't have to be just an older version of their younger selves. They can now be the New Old-Women!"

"What was the book called?"

"You know the title. *Aging in Babylon: The Sad Desperate Years of Nora Gray.*"

"Such a catchy title. You'd think I'd remember it."

"You remember it, all right. It was number one on the *New York Times* nonfiction best-seller list. I was on all the TV talk shows. It was critically acclaimed," she stated, as if Oprah's enthusiasm should end any discussion.

"What's it like to be a woman who knows everything?" I wondered. "It must give you an incredible sense of power to know how other women should dress, should feel, should love, should die."

"I have a point of view. A writer must have a point of view."

"I come from the movies, where the only point of view that matters is the camera's. I don't remember you interviewing me."

"You know I didn't. I talked to those who knew you best, including that young man . . . What was his name?"

"Magnus."

"That's right. English, wasn't he?"

"Yes. 'His hair was as black as a gigolo's pair of shoes,' " I quoted from memory.

"I wrote that. Not bad, if I do say so myself."

"Gigolo is such an old-fashioned-sounding word. And yet still so powerful."

She studied me for a second; it was all she needed. After all, Meg was a quick study. "Don't tell me you didn't know he was using you?" she sniffed.

"Magnus was kind."

"You paid him for his company."

"A monthly allowance. The least I could do."

"You got him a green card. You bought him clothes and a car. Did you honestly believe he was staying with you just for you, and not the perks you could offer him?"

"Magnus was kind."

"Women should not have to debase themselves for a few shreds of attention just because they grow old, because they lose their sexual potency," she pronounced.

"Magnus was kind."

"Would you stop saying that. I suppose he was kind to you in bed?"

"Yes."

"Kind can be condescending, especially in bed."

"Condescending can be condescending in or out of bed. Have you ever been in love?"

"There's been no Mr. Right."

"Then have you been in love with Mr. Wrong?"

"Many times. But I don't need men now. It's very freeing." She licked her papery lips. "Don't tell me you were in love with Magnus?"

"I think of myself as a pragmatic romantic."

"That's an oxymoron like bankers' trust," she scoffed, smiling her little weasel smile.

"When you are my age, and getting closer to death, you're more easily gratified and therefore more able to give. I've experienced the pain of rejection many times in my life. I know if I experience it again, I'll survive. I would've told you all this had you interviewed me. But instead you interviewed Magnus; he was so young and so easily hurt. He didn't know he could survive."

"The fact that you needed a Magnus says it all. Older women have to learn to protect themselves. And I don't mean by trying to look younger. Or having younger men. They need to become more of themselves. Wear baggy pantsuits. Let their hair go gray. Their stomachs hang out. Let youth go. Let men like Magnus go. Aging is letting go. Once we understand that, then we can't be hurt by it. And if you don't mind me saying so, let the mink coat go. It looks like something a fifties starlet would wear. You were a great actress. You didn't need to become a fag hag."

"That phrase, 'fag hag,' " I said. "It bewildered Magnus. He couldn't understand how he could be a gigolo and I could be a fag hag."

"Well, I'm sure you weren't paying him for his intelligence."

"No, his kindness."

"There's that word again."

"May I ask why you're in Silver Shadows?"

Keeping her back to me, Meg walked to the balustrade and stared down at the sweep of lawn and the cluster of quaint cottages we now called home. "The doctors tell me I'm too thin, emaciated actually. In other words I have an eating disorder."

"An aging actress is hard to digest," I murmured.

"What?" She turned, facing me.

"Managing stress helps you to digest."

"Spare me the platitudes. It's odd I should run into you here. I sometimes connect you to my eating disorder."

"Really?" This was news to me. My surprise was genuine.

"When I was young I wanted to look just like you," she confessed, bitterly. "I'd stare at myself in the mirror and suck in my cheekbones. I thought I'd die if I didn't look like you. And now you're sitting here . . ."

"A fag hag in an old silver mink coat?" I smiled, charmingly.

"I thought you had more backbone, more self-confidence, than to end up with some little out-of-work pretty-boy." She spit out the words.

"I didn't realize you had looked up to me when you were a girl."

"I looked up to Madame Curie. I said I wanted to look like you. There's a difference. You see, this is how society mistreats women. They make someone like you a symbol of beauty that no woman can possibly live up to."

"You don't seem that mistreated. You do have a book on the *New York Times* nonfiction best-seller list. And you've been on all the talk shows."

"You don't understand, do you? I wanted to be a foot taller. I wanted your long neck. I wanted your thinness."

"I've always been naturally thin. I can eat anything."

"I used to feel I was inadequate because of you."

"And so you end up writing a book to destroy me."

"No, to help other women." She eyed me with distrust. "Why are you in Silver Shadows?"

"Magnus." I moved the gun in my pocket so the barrel pointed at her.

"He left you?"

"Yes."

"You're better off. I suppose he left you for a young man, or another older wealthy woman?"

"I gave him a red Porsche Boxter. He drove it off a Malibu cliff. Sailed it right out over the Pacific Ocean toward the sun. A modern day Icarus. Except his goal wasn't to reach the sun. His goal was death."

"I'm sorry," she said, stiffly.

"His kindness was genuine until he read your book. Then he began to question his own good instincts. He began to feel not kind, but freakish. Where do women like you come from? Women who know everything?"

"Stop calling me a woman who knows everything. I'm an astute observer of our sex."

I smiled my famous wry smile. "Do you remember when we had G spots?"

"What spots?"

"G spots. We had them back in the seventies. They were part of our erogenous zone. It's not exactly something you'd think women would forget, but it seems that we have. Where are all the women who knew about G spots? Where did they go?"

"You blame me for Magnus's death, don't you?" she observed with all the perception of her craft.

We stared at each other. My hand tightened on the gun.

(*Acting Tip: Never rush the dramatic moment. Take your time. Allow for the pause, for a sense of the heart beating, the clock ticking. Allow for the sense of a life slipping away.*)

I said, "I blame you for being thoughtless and cruel. I blame you for thinking that you know everything. I blame you for being on the *New York Times* nonfiction best-seller list."

I released the safety catch.

"What was that noise?" she asked.

"What noise?"

"A clicking sound."

"I didn't hear it. Maybe the gardener is trimming the hedge over there."

"There is no gardener over there."

"Here you are, Meg." A young, perky, female attendant strolled onto the verandah carrying a large plastic glass filled with something pink and frothy.

(*Acting Tip: Always allow for the unexpected by staying in the present, the moment. Never break your focus, your concentration. Let the other actors fall out of character and flounder and flop like beached whales.*)

"Now I want you to drink this malt all down," the attendant instructed Meg, placing the pink drink on the table next to her.

"It's enormous." Meg turned green sizing up her drink.

"It's yummy," the attendant coaxed.

"I can't drink it if you're going to watch me."

"All right." She beamed at me. "How are you, Miss Gray?"

"Fine." My hand around the gun was sweating.

"You must be warm?"

"Not in the least."

"Even animals shed their fur, Miss Gray." She tilted her relentlessly cheerful face into Meg's. "No more feeding the potted palms with this stuff or you'll get an IV in your arm tonight." She swished off.

Meg glared at the giant malt.

"Aren't you going to drink it?"

"No. Why?"

"You are thin."

"I know that intellectually. But I don't really know it. I can't see it. Even in the mirror. I can't process it. Such an odd position for me to be in."

"For a woman who knows everything," I said, noticing, for the first time, the dark circles under her eyes and the pallor of her dry translucent skin.

"The thought of drinking this is making me ill. Where the hell am I going to throw it so they won't see it? They always check up on me."

"What's in your drink?"

"Vanilla ice cream, eggs, honey, milk, berries. Vitamins." She could barely say the words without physically recoiling.

It was then I realized that Meg was devouring herself. Living off her own body. Meg West was dying.

(*Acting Tip: When you experience a revelation about another character that changes your predetermined course of action, you must go with it. This will give your performance a sense of spontaneity, and keep the other actors on their toes.*)

I put the safety catch back on.

"There's that clicking sound again. Are you making it?" she demanded, irritably. "It goes right through me."

I let the gun slide back down into the hem of my coat.

"I'll drink your malt for you," I offered, graciously.

"Why?" she asked, ungraciously.

"I'm hungry. You're not."

"You won't tell? I don't want an IV stuck in me tonight."

"I won't tell."

"Is this an act of kindness?" she questioned.

"You really don't know what kindness is, do you?" I answered, shedding my coat and taking her drink.

(*Acting Tip: You must never forget your goal in a scene, even though your method of attaining that goal has changed. In other words, there is more than one way to skin a cat.*)

M. D. Lake is a two-time Agatha winner for his short stories, "Kim's Game" and "Tea for Two," and writes a mystery series featuring campus cop Peggy O'Neill, including Death Calls the Tune. *In this story, Lake draws a love quadrangle that spells out some distinct complications for its participants.*

A. B. C. D. E. A. T. H.

M. D. Lake

Andrew, Brenda, Chuck, and Debbie. The Alphabetical Order, their friends called them, as in "Let's not forget to invite the Alphabetical Order," or "Oh, look! Here comes the Alphabetical Order!"

Andrew was Andrew Macallister, professor of international studies at the University, and Brenda, his wife, was Brenda Byrd-Macallister, a professor of comparative literature who needs no introduction to those of you familiar with advanced literary theory and can tell the difference between Derrida and Dairy Queen. They were in their late forties, poised, sophisticated, always smartly dressed and with that lush silver hair so admired in academia. They looked younger than their years, for they worked out regularly at an expensive health club.

Chuck was Chuck Partridge, an artist who'd gained a fleeting national reputation for a series of paintings that featured the private parts of the subjects of famous works of art, his *Mona Lisa* being perhaps the most notorious. His wife, Debbie, was an author who, under the pen name Cherilynn Twain, wrote moderately successful romance novels of the steamier kind.

Chuck and Debbie were some twenty years younger than Andrew and Brenda and they looked the way you'd expect people to look who spent their working days wrestling with their Muse of choice. Chuck's hair was long and unkempt and he somehow managed to keep a day's growth of beard on his face, God knows how. Debbie's photograph can be found on the back covers of her books, where the camera appears to have surprised her trying to inhale a large, sensuous flower, so if you're interested in what she looked like, you can check your local used bookstores.

Despite the differences in age, education, status, and personality, Andrew and Brenda, Chuck and Debbie, were best friends, attracted to what they saw in the other that they felt they lacked in themselves.

Too attracted, it turned out, for after several years Andrew and Debbie fell in love, as did Chuck and Brenda. A, D, C, and B, now. Alphabetical Disorder, Alphabet Soup. But they were discreet and neither their mates nor their friends ever had a clue.

Why did they fall so fatally in love, you ask, the two coolly elegant and well-groomed academics and the passionate, somewhat hirsute, artists? How can anybody answer a question like that with any certainty!

It might have been because both Andrew and Brenda

had recently suffered setbacks in their careers. Andrew's long awaited book on Soviet politics, in which he'd argued with irrefutable logic that the Soviet Union could only be brought down through a nuclear war that would destroy the world, had unfortunately come out the week before the Soviet Union tumbled down without a nuclear device being detonated or a shot fired. Andrew became a laughingstock in his field (you know how cruel academic critics can be), although his job wasn't threatened, for he had tenure.

Brenda, his wife, wasn't as lucky. Her specialty within comparative literature was irony, which she found in the most remarkable places, including, in an article just published in a distinguished journal, the "Lord's Prayer." Under normal circumstances such an article would not have raised an eyebrow within her field—indeed, it would have advanced her career. But she didn't have tenure, and the chairman of her department, who did, had recently become a born-again Christian. As a result, Brenda's professional future was clouded, for born-again Christians frown on irony, especially when applied to biblical texts.

These setbacks, going, as they did, against all logic, seriously undermined the intellectual and (dare we say it, in this cynical, secular age?) moral foundations of Andrew and Brenda, which may help explain why they threw themselves so unreservedly into the arms of their best friends' mates.

Why Chuck, the painter, and Debbie, the romance writer, returned the passion of the two academics is more of a mystery. But, as they themselves would be the first to insist, why ask? It's perhaps enough to say that they were artists, and artists have always behaved irresponsibly.

Andrew and Brenda taught only on Monday, Wednesday, and Friday, so Andrew could spend all of Tuesday and Thursday in Debbie's arms, in the ramshackle little house she shared with Chuck on the outskirts of town, and

Brenda could spend those same days at Chuck's studio, where he kept a futon on the floor for those nights when, after an arduous day spent spewing his demons onto canvas, he was too exhausted to go home. At first Debbie and Andrew worried about Chuck coming home early and catching them in the act, just as Chuck and Brenda worried about Debbie dropping in on Chuck at his studio unexpectedly. But that never happened. Obviously.

As mentioned somewhere above, they were discreet. It might be expressed like this: A hadn't the foggiest idea how B was spending her Tuesdays and Thursdays, and C had no idea how D was spending hers. And vice versa. Alphabetically it was a mess, but none of them thought so: they were having the time of their lives.

"I can't believe it!" Andrew—or maybe it was Chuck—exclaimed one afternoon with a laugh, in the afterglow of sex. "I'm having an affair with my best friend's wife! It's such a cliché!" Andrew, the professor, and Chuck, the artist, had spent their lives trying to avoid clichés. They had that in common, at least.

"But how could you ever get to know your worst enemy's wife well enough to fall in love with her?" replied the ironic Brenda—or was it the romantic Debbie?

They laughed at that, whichever couple it was—or maybe all four of them laughed at it at about the same time, as they lay sprawled on the bed (in one case) and the futon (in the other), their limbs entwined (in both cases).

Oh, but they could get serious too sometimes, don't think they couldn't! And, on occasion, almost profound. To give you one example, they expressed the belief (the academics probably started it) that they'd been living in marriages that were too one-sided: Andrew and Brenda had been living too much in their heads while neglecting the irrational and emotional aspects of their natures—the "Dionysian," Brenda liked to call it, which confused

Chuck at first, until she explained what the term meant—
while Chuck and Debbie, not to be outdone, mused that
they'd neglected the rational and intellectual in their natures, the development of which is so necessary to living
fully balanced lives. "The Apollonian," Andrew supplied,
then cleared up Debbie's bewilderment with a helpful def-
inition. Until fairly recently, Andrew had flattered himself
that he looked a bit like Apollo—an unusually serene and
clear-sighted god—but no longer, since he felt it unlikely
that Apollo was ever in the arms of a woman like Debbie,
or would have wanted to be.

And time passed.

It was inevitable that sometimes they would lie in bed
(or, in the case of Brenda and Chuck, on the futon) and discuss their marriages, and not surprisingly they agreed that
these seemed to be getting less endurable with each passing Tuesday and Thursday.

It was equally inevitable that the talk would turn to divorce.

"No!" Andrew and Brenda protested firmly, as one. "A
love such as ours can only exist underground, can only
thrive in secrecy!" After so many years of trusting in reason alone, they found it hard to put their trust in anything
else. After all, they had Ph.D.'s.

"Oh, you're so wrong!" cried Chuck and Debbie, their
voices throbbing with—what else?—passion. They had
only one high school diploma between them, earned
through a correspondence school which advertised on the
inside of matchbooks. "That's the problem with the world
today," they went on. "The emotions, which are really *very*
healthy, are suppressed until they finally wither and die."

Could it be true? wondered Andrew and Brenda, and,
letting some of their colleagues pass in review through
their minds, concluded that it could.

Andrew and Brenda whined, "But I'm twenty years

older than you! When I'm in my sixties, you'll only be my age now. You'll tire of me."

"Love is all that matters!" asserted Chuck and Debbie ardently. They were young and knew nothing yet of time and its ravages, so they almost certainly believed what they were saying.

"There's a problem, though," Andrew and Brenda said, late one Tuesday or Thursday afternoon, as they were dressing in preparation to return to their dreary homes and equally dreary mates in Faculty Grove.

"And what's that?" asked Chuck and Debbie, rolling their eyes in exasperation at the obstacles the other two were forever throwing in the way of true love.

"Don't you see?" Andrew said. "If I divorce Brenda, the courts might award her half my salary—especially as she's soon apt to lose her job on account of that damned article she wrote on the 'Lord's Prayer.' And if you divorce Chuck, he might end up with half your income. You say yourself that you live in fear of hearing from your agent that your series has been canceled, now that women with marginal reading skills are turning to the Internet and away from the romance novel."

And Brenda said: "Don't you see? If I divorce Andrew, the courts might award me nothing—and I'm almost certainly going to lose my job soon. And if you divorce Debbie, she might end up with half your income, which you say yourself has shrunk considerably, as people become numb to the outrages you commit in acrylic on canvas."

Andrew and Brenda summed up what was bothering them in words that, for academics, were unusually succinct: "We could all end up poor."

Even the enthusiasm of the two romantics was briefly dampened at hearing those words, but their happy moods soon revived and the weeks passed, the brightly colored Tuesdays and Thursdays shadowed by the unbearably gray

Mondays, Wednesdays, Fridays, Saturdays, and Sundays.

They began fantasizing about the deaths of their mates: "A sudden, quickly progressing illness," mused Andrew and Brenda, though perhaps not in exactly the same words. "Or an accident—as painless as possible. It would be dreadful, of course, but it would solve the problem."

"What problem?" wondered Chuck and Debbie aloud, their minds on other things.

Now it was the turn of the two academics to roll their eyes in exasperation. "The money problem, of course," they snapped.

"Oh, yeah, that. And how would a fatal accident solve the money problem?"

"The University," Andrew and Brenda explained patiently, "gives its professors large insurance policies, and of course we have additional insurance of our own."

While it was a deplorable fact, they went on, that their mates were worth much more to them dead than alive, it would be a terrible thing if anything happened to them. "We mustn't even fantasize about it," they concluded.

But they did, all four of them, each in his or her own way. How could they not?

One afternoon, Chuck and Debbie brought up the subject of murder. As a joke? Who knows! They might not have known themselves, since introspection, as all but the most obtuse reader must have realized by now, wasn't their strong suit.

Andrew and Brenda shuddered. "What a horrible thought," they exclaimed quickly. Too quickly? Perhaps.

"Besides," they added—chorused, actually, although they didn't realize it—"it wouldn't work."

"Why not?" the other two chimed in antiphonally from different parts of town, different sorts of bed.

"The spouse is the first person the police suspect."

Debbie and Chuck brooded awhile about that. "Unless,"

they whispered, between caresses and kisses, "I were to do it for you and you for me."

Well, there was a thought!

"Oh!" the two academics protested, aghast. "Murder would change everything! We would have to live the rest of our lives with the knowledge that we had blood on our hands. Murderers always sleep uneasily—especially if the person they're sleeping with is a murderer too."

Chuck and Debbie weren't convinced of that, or else didn't see it as a serious obstacle to living happily ever after, but they didn't say anything, and all four ended up agreeing that they'd just have to go on as they were, "stealing time out of time," as Debbie, the one with the most emotive language skills, so beautifully expressed it, and hoping that an accident would befall their mates—not too terribly painful, of course, but fatal.

And so the affairs continued for a few more weeks.

Then, one Thursday afternoon, as he lay in bed with Debbie, Andrew happened to mention that he was obliged to attend an emergency faculty meeting that night, to discuss the University's current budgetary crisis, this one caused by the enormous salary increase recently given the football coach to keep him from going elsewhere. The meeting promised, he said with an exaggerated groan, to be long and boring. Brenda wouldn't be home until late that night either, he added, almost as if speaking to himself, since she taught an evening class on Thursdays. As if Debbie didn't already know that!

And Debbie, probably only for something to say between bouts of lovemaking, told Andrew that she was having dinner with a bunch of old high school friends that night at Le Petit Coucou, an amusing little bistro in an equally amusing part of town. Later, in some other context, she mentioned that Chuck would also be eating out that night with friends, at Picasso's Armpit, a bar and grill much frequented by artists that was in the same amusing, if poorly lit, neighborhood as Le Petit Coucou.

At about the same time, on the futon in Chuck's studio on the other side of town, Brenda was staring up at the ceiling and telling Chuck the same story about her plans for the evening, and she just happened to mention Andrew's plans too. Chuck, a little later, perhaps only to fill a silence that had grown up between them, also told her his and Debbie's evening plans.

If you wonder at this, it's probably an indication that you don't know a great deal about the steamier affairs of the heart. Lovers, after all, have to do something during those moments (which can occasionally stretch into minutes and even longer) when the tide of desire is temporarily out, and most often what they do is make idle chitchat, and that's probably all this was: idle chitchat. It doesn't have to have any deeper significance.

But it did start the four lovers thinking.

Chuck and Debbie (not surprisingly, given their natures) had already decided they were going to murder Andrew and Brenda, and they intended to do it in such a way that their lovers wouldn't know they'd done it, for Andrew and Brenda, they felt, were too civilized to participate in anything so barbarous, and so final. Oh, they might suspect the truth, yes, but they wouldn't know for sure, and that would make all the difference. Academics can live with uncertainty—in fact, they can't live without it, at least those affiliated with the better universities.

Debbie realized that Andrew would have a cast-iron alibi that night if she murdered Brenda while he was safely wrapped up in his budget meeting. Therefore, as soon as Andrew was out the door that afternoon, she called her best friend and, pleading illness, canceled her dinner engagement at Le Petit Coucou. She planned to shoot Brenda with the nickel-plated automatic that, on account of the bad neighborhood in which she lived and wrote, she kept for self-defense.

Chuck realized that Brenda would have a solid alibi that night with her class, thus giving him the perfect opportunity to murder Andrew. He planned to do this with the revolver he'd kept in his studio ever since an art lover, temporarily deranged at the sight of one of his more despicable paintings, had tried to choke him to death. He didn't bother calling his friends to tell them he wouldn't be joining them for dinner at Picasso's Armpit, for artists are notoriously unreliable and he knew his friends would understand.

Meanwhile, as she drove away from Chuck's studio, Brenda reflected on the fact that Chuck would have a cast-iron alibi that night with his artist friends at Picasso's Armpit. After a few moments of agonizing inner turmoil, she convinced herself that this would be a perfect opportunity to kill two birds with one stone (a hackneyed image she would not have used herself): not only to murder Debbie, but also to rid herself, once and for all, of the ironic mask she'd worn for so long to conceal from herself her fear of life in all its naked immediacy. She called her department and, pleading a family emergency, canceled her evening class, then drove downtown and bought a Saturday night special from a man standing on a street corner who she thought—correctly, as it turned out—might sell them.

Andrew, in his turn, as he drove away from Debbie's little house, pondered the fact that Debbie would have an unshakable alibi that night with her friends at Le Petit Coucou. He concluded that if he was ever going to throw off his reflective nature and become a man of action, now was the time to do it. Accordingly, he called his department chairman and, hacking and coughing loudly into the phone, informed him that he was too ill to attend the budget meeting that night. Then he drove home and retrieved from the attic the expensive shotgun he'd purchased some years before, when he'd thought, erroneously, that shooting grouse would be the antidote he was looking for to the strenuous intellectual labor demanded by his profession.

And so, hours later, there they were, once again in alphabetical order: Andrew skulking nervously in a nasty-smelling alley next to Picasso's Armpit, Brenda huddled in the shelter of a pawnshop's awning across the street from Le Petit Coucou, Chuck lurking in the shadows of the building in which Andrew's department was holding its budget meeting, and Debbie crouched in the shrubbery outside the building in which Brenda taught—*and they were all armed!*

"It's going to be the perfect crime," they thought simultaneously, or nearly so, as they shivered and waited on that chill and overcast night for their chosen prey.

Time passed, it began to rain, a cold, steady rain, and their victims failed to appear.

Finally Andrew, tired of waiting in the alley with the shotgun concealed in his raincoat, forced himself to enter the dark and smoky Picasso's Armpit, where he ascertained that Chuck was not there; Brenda, her purse heavy with the Saturday night special, splashed across the street to Le Petit Coucou, entered, looked around, and couldn't see Debbie anywhere; Chuck, in the campus shadows, nervously spinning his revolver's cylinder, overheard one plump academic remark to another as they emerged from Andrew's building that Andrew was a lucky dog for having come down with the flu and been unable to attend the meeting; and Debbie—growing impatient and wet on the other side of campus and tired of flicking her automatic's safety on and off—accosted a student leaving Brenda's building and was told that Professor Byrd-Macallister had canceled her class, pleading a family emergency.

Frustrated and annoyed—even, perhaps, a little indignant, and certainly cold and wet—Andrew and Brenda hastened to Chuck and Debbie's run-down little house in its shabby neighborhood, hoping to find their lovers' mates there in time to murder them while they still had the nerve, even as Chuck and Debbie rushed to Andrew and Brenda's lovely home in Faculty Grove on a similar deplorable errand. They were all in such a hurry, in fact, that Andrew and Brenda, their cars parked in the same atmospherically-lit block near the two eateries, almost collided in their single-minded need to get to their cars, while Chuck and Debbie, as they left the University, failed to recognize each another as their paths crossed on the mall, poorly lit on account of the budget crisis mentioned earlier.

So close did this story come to being a comedy.

They met at their lovers' doors. Andrew mistook the dark shape on the porch trying to enter Debbie's house for Chuck, while Brenda, casting a furtive glance over her shoulder, thought the figure rushing up Chuck's walk behind her, raincoat flapping, shotgun pointing, was Debbie; across town, Chuck thought—well, we know what Chuck thought. And Debbie too.

Shots rang out. Two here, two there.

There's very little left to tell. Eventually, of course, the police arrived, summoned by concerned neighbors. At one of the homes, a young cop scratched his head as he contemplated the mess (corrupting, incidentally, the crime scene with dandruff, for which he'd be given a stern talking-to later) and remarked, "They don't look like they belong in a neighborhood like this, do they, Sarge? Whaddaya think's the story?"

At that scene or maybe the other one, the sergeant—older, wiser, and close to retirement—growled, "I ain't

paid to think, son, but take my word for it: when all's said
and done, it'll turn out to be the same old story. It's always
the same old story, as simple as ABC."

How Andrew and Brenda, Chuck and Debbie, would
have hated hearing that!

Martha C. Lawrence was nominated for Agatha, Edgar, and Anthony awards for her first book, featuring parapsychologist Elizabeth Chase, Murder in Scorpio. *This novel was followed by* The Cold Heart of Capricorn, Aquarius Descending, *and* Pisces Rising. *Related to Lawrence's interest in psychic phenomena, her story tells of a cave in La Jolla which holds an irresistable attraction for several people . . .*

The Sea Cave

Martha C. Lawrence

High on a majestic sandstone cliff along the La Jolla coast sits a local landmark called The Cave Store. It's been there for a hundred odd years, which makes it ancient by California standards. Nestled in a drift of fir needles and shaded by windswept Torrey pines, the shop commands a jaw-dropping vista of the Pacific Ocean. The view is literally worth a million, but the store's main attraction lies inside, where Dora Panella sits near the cash register, leafing through *The National Enquirer.* Brassy-haired and peren-

nially thirty-nine, the clerk has long since become inured
to the enchanting locale. She started the job with high
hopes, envisioning romantic encounters with wealthy
tourists. Three years of broken dreams and lousy wages
have dulled her appreciation for the ocean view, not to
mention the sea cave.

"Why do they call this The Cave Store?"

Dora, chewing thoughtfully on a wad of gum, is so engrossed in her reading that she doesn't realize the customer
is speaking to her.

"Excuse me . . . ma'am?"

She pulls herself away from a story on the latest
celebrity nose jobs and looks up to see a man leaning on a
cane. He's fairly young—forty at most—the picture of a
proper southern gentleman in his white linen suit. Dora
thinks it a pity that the image is ruined by a long, graying
ponytail cascading over his left shoulder. The man gives her
a smile and makes a sweep of the shop with his free hand.

"Will you please explain where you get the name for this
place? Golly, just look at all the light pourin' in these windows! Doesn't look anything like a cave."

Texas, Dora thinks. *Only men from Texas use words like
golly.* She gives the man a tight smile and tries her best not
to sound as if she's answered the question twenty thousand
times before.

"Take a look at the far wall over there." Dora waits while
the man turns toward the back of the shop. "Behind that
door is a tunnel that goes all the way down through the cliff
to a big cave that opens at the sea."

"You're pullin' my leg."

"You can see for yourself, if you have two dollars and
the energy to climb back up a hundred forty-four stairs."
Dora looks down at the man's cane, doubting very much
that Mr. Gimpy will try it. When she looks up, he meets her
gaze with piercing gray eyes.

"I just might do that."

She shrugs and returns to her *National Enquirer,* hoping the man won't ask for a coffee drink. Her job was a lot easier before the espresso maker went in. People used to come in and just look at the cave, maybe buy a souvenir or something. These days she's expected to be a waitress *and* a busboy, for the same insulting hourly rate. She resents the machine so much that every now and then she'll dip behind the counter and spit into the lattes. Makes it so much easier to smile when she hands the coffee to customers.

"Is that a picture of the sea cave there?"

He's asking about the creepy painting hanging on the back wall. It is indeed a picture of the famous sea cave, rendered in murky oils. Dora answers without even looking up from the *Enquirer*'s before-and-after photos of Hollywood's most notable noses.

"Yeah, that's the cave. But the painting's not for sale."

Mr. Gimpy nods and directs his attention to the jewelry under the glass countertop. Dora sees from his smirk that he's unimpressed, and her opinion of him goes up a notch. A lot of people who looked like they ought to know better gushed over the "curios"—tarnished cigarette lighters, out-of-date earrings, scratched cuff links, and the like. Robert, her endlessly irritating boss, purchases the junk for practically nothing at estate sales and auctions and marks up each piece for resale eight, sometimes nine hundred percent. Dora is at once appalled and impressed by his shamelessness. "It's the setting and ambiance that add value," Robert often said in that snotty voice of his. "People want to take home a piece of California."

Mr. Gimpy pulls a wallet from the inside pocket of his jacket and places a five dollar bill on the glass countertop.

"It sounds like a heck of a phenomenon, that old sea cave. I guess I gotta go and see this thing. Does it have a name or anything?"

"They call it Sunny Jim Cave." Dora opens the cash register and stows the five. "Created by centuries of waves pounding into that sandstone down there."

"So Sunny Jim's the boy who dug the tunnel?"

"No. Sunny Jim's just a nickname." This is the one part of Dora's job that she truly enjoys, knowing the store's history and conveying it to customers. She likes having ready answers, and wishes she could always feel so smart. "The tunnel was built in 1902 by a German-born geologist named Gustav Shutz. He recognized the tourist potential of the spot and hired two Chinese laborers away from local opium smugglers. Put 'em to work digging through the cliff with picks and shovels."

"Picks and shovels?" Mr. Gimpy's eyes widen as he takes his three dollars in change. "That must've taken darn near forever!"

"Two years." Dora shifts the gum from one side of her mouth to the other. "They added the stairs later, no one really knows for sure when."

The man looks genuinely impressed. He leans against his cane and shoves his change into his pants pocket before heading to the back of the store. When he reaches the tunnel door, he pokes his head in and turns back to Dora.

"Kinda spooky, ain't it?"

"It's lighted all the way to the sea. Just gets a little damp about halfway down, so watch your step." Dora keeps an eye on his white suit as it disappears into the dim tunnel. "Take it easy on those middle stairs," she calls after him. But she isn't really concerned. In spite of his cane, Mr. Gimpy moves as nimbly as a cat.

Dora turns again to her gossip rag, but she's gotten the gist of the story from the photos and reading seems like too much trouble. She pushes the paper aside, thinking that the man was right. The cave is pretty spooky. A wicked smile crosses her face. Maybe in a few minutes she'll turn out the lights down there, just to give him a scare. But walking over to the light switch is too much of a bother. Dora stays put, staring out the store's west-facing windows. Far below, the jagged white lines of breaking ocean waves look like string floating in a giant bathtub; the surfboards and occasional kayak bobbing on the swells look like bath toys.

The front door opens, setting the copper bells on the doorjamb jangling. A warning system of sorts, along with the closed-circuit television mounted at the entrance. Dora sits up straighter when she recognizes Robert coming into the shop. Large-boned and portly, her boss makes an intimidating entrance, the heels of his Italian boots thumping across the hardwood floor. He approaches the counter wearing a self-satisfied grin. Robert doesn't smile often, so his good mood makes her wary. He doesn't bother with a hello.

"Is Craig around?"

Dora bites back a sarcastic reply, as she often does when the subject of Robert's younger brother comes up.

"Haven't seen him."

"That's odd. He was supposed to be helping you out today."

No, Dora thinks, *that's not odd, that's typical.* For all his fancy college degrees and expensive cars, the boss's brother is a no-count speed junkie. Even before she found out for certain, Dora guessed it by Craig's sunken cheeks, restless eyes, and the way he wore long-sleeved shirts— usually black—no matter how hot the weather.

"Maybe he got his days mixed up," she says.

"No." Robert is irritated with her, Dora can tell by the tone of his voice. "I just saw him at lunchtime. He was really excited when I showed him what I found at auction this morning. Said he'd be helping you at the shop later today."

Craig said a lot of things, most of them lies. When Dora found his little bag of goodies—hypo, spoon, cotton balls, the works—she dangled it in front of his face and kidded him that she was going to tell his big brother. Craig snatched it away and flew into one of his red-faced rages, calling her a proletarian cow. That night Dora looked up "proletarian" in the dictionary, and she'd hated Craig ever since. Not that she was overly fond of Robert.

"So it was a good day at auction, huh?" She smiles, making a weak attempt to be friendly. Robert simply glares at her.

"How many times do I have to tell you, Dora, that you *cannot* chew gum while you're working with customers? We have an image to keep up."

And you have your head up, she thinks.

"Sorry. I'm trying to quit cigarettes and the gum really helps." She knows the boss doesn't approve of the cleavage peeking out of her double-knit top, either, and wonders if he'll have the nerve to mention it.

He cocks an eyebrow at her *National Enquirer* and shakes his head as if she's a hopeless cause. She decides not to give him the satisfaction of getting to her.

"So, why was Craig excited about the auction today?" she asks.

The grin returns to Robert's face. He flops a buttery calf-skin bag onto the glass countertop.

"Wait until you see this."

Robert unbuckles a side flap pocket and reaches into the bag. He pauses dramatically, looking at her with shining eyes.

"Ready?"

Dora nods, curious now. Robert pulls his hand from the bag and opens his fist. Dora stares at his outstretched palm.

"What is it?"

"This is an historical treasure! Look." He holds the thing

to the light pouring through the west-facing window. "It absolutely, positively *glows*. You just don't see this kind of beauty and refinement in the jewelry they make today."

Dora leans over for a closer look. The brooch is shaped like a butterfly. Its body is made from the largest, most lustrous pearl she's ever seen. The wings are flowing planes of glittering diamonds, tipped with rubies and dotted by four perfect emeralds. Dora wonders if anyone even wears brooches anymore.

"How old is it?" she asks.

"Old as the Civil War. This piece was probably crafted around 1863. Brooches like these were all the rage back then."

"That looks like it might actually be worth something."

"Would you like to hold it?"

Dora nods and holds out her palm. From the paranoid way Robert places the brooch in her hand, he's acting like it's a radioactive bomb or something.

"Be *very* careful. I just had that piece appraised for fifty-five thousand dollars, give or take a few hundred. The old woman who owned this brooch died without a will or any heirs, poor dear. I picked it up for a song, comparatively speaking."

The butterfly feels surprisingly heavy in Dora's palm. She stares at its sparkling diamond wings, thinking about the freedom that even half of fifty-five thousand dollars could buy her.

Robert sees the desire in her gaze and gives her a stern look. He holds his own palm open, rather impatiently, Dora thinks, and waits for her to return the brooch. As soon as the jewel is in his hand, he snatches it out of sight.

"This one doesn't even go on display." He walks over to the wall at the back of the shop and lifts the painting of the sea cave off its hook, revealing the safe hidden behind it. He stands with his back to Dora, pointedly blocking her view as he spins the safe dial. "I've made a few discreet calls. I have a customer coming in for a private viewing of the brooch tomorrow morning. Finds like this don't come along often."

Dora wishes Robert had a latte she could spit in. Does he have to be so blatant about not trusting her? If she were a thief, she would've already robbed him. She knows the combination to that safe. She stumbled across it weeks ago, when she was cleaning under the cash drawer. Three numbers in Robert's tight, squarish hand, written on the back of one of his business cards. On a hunch, Dora took her first opportunity alone to spin the safe's dial, using those numbers. Her heart jumped when she felt the tumblers fall; blood rushed to her face when she opened the safe door and saw the modest bundle of bills inside. She left the money untouched. Scared she'd get caught, mainly. But still, he didn't have to treat her like a common thief.

Robert turns around and catches the frown on her face.

"Oh, come on, don't be offended. Craig offered to keep the butterfly in his safety deposit box, but I wouldn't even trust my own brother with this thing." He laughs, as if it's a joke. Dora doesn't see anything funny about it.

"I wouldn't trust Craig, either."

Robert scowls and snaps:

"I'm kidding, Dora. My brother *has* the combination to this safe, for heaven's sake. I trust him explicitly." He freezes, as if he's just remembered something.

"Dora . . ." His voice trails off.

"Yeah?"

Robert's eyes bore suspiciously into hers.

"Craig said you once boasted that you knew the combination to this safe. Is that true?"

Dora smacks her gum and lets out a nervous laugh.

"I wish!" She laughs some more. "No way. I was just kidding around."

The boss continues to stare at her with narrowed eyes. Gradually, he mellows out.

"Hey, why don't you relax, take the rest of the day off . . . close up a little early tonight?"

Dora wants to puke, the way Robert says it, like he's doing her some big favor. She knows perfectly well he's just trying to get rid of her.

"Can't leave yet. There's one last customer in the cave."

"Oh." He crosses his arms over his chest, looking annoyed. "Well, when that customer leaves, go ahead and lock up, all right?"

Dora shrugs.

"Sure, whatever."

Robert walks out without saying good-bye, slamming the door behind him. The bells on the doorjamb complain and grow quiet. Soon the shop is completely silent, save for the ghostly sighs of the waves far below. Dora stares at the creepy painting of the sea cave as if she can see right through it, and begins to scheme.

Two hundred feet below, Craig navigates his kayak through the smooth water beyond the breakers and looks toward the sea cave. He shakes his head. *How many damn fools have paid good money to walk through that dank tunnel in the last hundred years?* he wonders. The shadows of a pair of black cormorants cross his face and he looks up. His eyes follow the birds as they land on the narrow sandstone ridge just above the cave's gaping entrance. The sun is setting and the breeze is colder than the ocean water's sixty-five degrees.

Inside his wet suit, Craig is feeling neither cold nor pain.

He picks up the long, tapering stiletto from the floor of

the kayak and tucks the knife into his dive belt. He knows that half the time, Dora forgets to close the door to the tunnel when she locks up. The door is secured by a simple latch, so if she happens to close it tonight, he can open it easily enough by pushing the slender blade up between the door and the frame. He smiles, thinking about Robert's diamond butterfly sitting in that safe, and how perfectly easy this little raid will be. By coming up through the cave, he'll run no risk of witnesses, including the lens of the security camera out front. He'll be in and out and fifty grand richer. Robert will never suspect him. The blame for the robbery will fall on that lazy bitch. Then Robert will *have* to fire her—a double bonus.

Craig paddles closer. A white form appears from the black mouth of the cave and for a minute Craig thinks he's tripping on a ghost. No, it's a man, all right, in a white suit, leaning on a cane. Craig watches him make his way to the edge of the wooden platform that juts from the floor of the cave out over the waves. The man stands there for several minutes, looking out to sea.

Craig pulls back the sleeve of his wet suit and glances at his watch. In fifteen minutes Dora will be closing the store, which means the man with the cane will have to climb back up the tunnel stairs soon. He puts his oar into the ocean and spins the kayak around. He'll be back.

Dora walks to the back of the shop. She has it all figured out. She knows a guy who fences high-end merchandise and cars, has been doing it for years. It's entirely possible that he'll get her twenty, twenty-five thousand dollars for the diamond butterfly, if it's worth what Robert says it is. She can cut the power to the security camera, make it look like a break-in. She stares at the ugly painting, itching to open the safe door behind it.

When she hears the last customer's footsteps echoing

up from the open door to the tunnel, her smile is genuine. *Finally.*

"Hey!" she calls down. "How'd you like the cave?"

Mr. Gimpy's face has a healthy flush, but in spite of the cane, he isn't even out of breath.

"It was terrific! Best thing I've seen in California since those big red trees up north."

As soon as he reaches the top stair, Dora ushers him toward the exit, eager to be rid of him.

"Glad you enjoyed it. Hope you can visit again sometime."

Halfway across the shop the man stops, a troubled look on his face.

"But you know what? The sides of that cave are weeping, have you ever noticed that?"

Dora dismisses his comment with a flick of her wrist.

"That's just water, seeping through the sandstone."

Mr. Gimpy puts a hand on her arm.

"It's more than water, my dear." He gets a funny look in his eye. "Has anything . . . *unseemly* ever happened in that tunnel? Because I get a real dark feeling from it."

Something in his tone gives Dora pause.

"What do you mean, unseemly?"

"Frightening."

Dora thinks back to what she knows of the tunnel's history.

"Not really. Once in a while a surfer gets caught in the cave at high tide. A couple of them have had to spend the night in the tunnel. Is that what you mean?"

Mr. Gimpy doesn't answer. He just stands there leaning on his cane, a frown wrinkling his forehead. Dora impatiently checks her watch, wishing he'd get going. At last he speaks.

"I'd like to tell you something, but . . ." He doesn't finish the sentence. Dora hates it when people do that.

"What?" She's short with him and sounds rude, but doesn't care.

"I'm a psychic," he says matter-of-factly. "I saw something disturbing when I was in the cave."

Dora laughs with relief. The guy's a nutso. She should've known.

"Well I hope whatever you saw doesn't give you nightmares." Dora feels like she's talking to a child. Her mind goes back to grown-up thoughts. She looks back at the painting of the sea cave, eager to open the door of the safe and seize the treasure inside. "Listen, it's closing time. I've got to lock up now."

He puts his hand on her arm again, this time giving her sleeve a little tug.

"I saw *you*, I'm afraid. You were thinking about opening a door you mustn't open."

Shit, Dora thinks, *he can read my mind!*

"You mustn't do it. That's the message I was gettin' down there, real strong. You mustn't open that door or something terrible's gonna happen."

Dora does her best to pretend she doesn't know what he's talking about.

"What door?"

"All I can tell you is that there's a door, and this door is meant to stay closed. If it opens, there'll be trouble. Now, I don't know if that means anything to you or not, but please think about it, would you?"

"Uh, sure." His gray eyes are staring at Dora so intently that she has to look away. Outside, the sun has dropped behind the sea and the red horizon is fading into smoky-colored clouds. She sighs impatiently.

"I don't mean to rush you, sir, but I really gotta be closing now."

"I won't keep you, then."

He makes his way to the exit. When he reaches it, he

turns back as if to say something. Dora knows that he wants to warn her about opening the safe again. She gives him a strained smile. He smiles back, but his eyes are sad.

"Y'all take care, now." With that, he's gone.

Once the customer is out of sight, Dora loses no time. She puts the Closed sign in the window and hurries through her nightly chores: cashing out the register, wiping down the glass countertop, tidying up the bathroom. The tasks give her time to think about the consequences of stealing the diamond brooch. What if they can prove she's stolen it? She'll lose her job, go to jail.

She remembers a pair of gloves in her coat pockets. She'll leave no prints. As long as she cuts the power to the security monitor, no one will see her. They'll have nothing but circumstantial evidence. She'll make more money in one day than Robert would pay her in a year.

Damn if I'm going to let some psychic spook me.

She digs the gloves from her coat pockets and puts them on as she hurries to the fuse box. She flips the switch that cuts power to the front of the shop. The light above the door goes out and the security monitor goes black. She hurries to the back of the shop, pushes the sea cave painting aside, and spins the dial of the safe. That's when she notices how fast her heart is beating. Her tongue feels fuzzy. She really could use a drink of water.

Dora forgets about her thirst as soon as she swings open the safe door and holds the jeweled butterfly in her palm. Even in the half-lighted shop, the brooch is more beautiful than she remembered it. Was it really made during the Civil War? She wonders who was the first to wear it. Was she a Southern belle, or the wife of a wealthy Northerner? *Who cares?* Dora thinks with a smile. *It's mine now.*

Something—a sound—interrupts her thoughts. Dora holds her breath. Yes, there it is again: footsteps, coming up the tunnel stairs.

Damn! Of all the days for a surfer to get trapped in the cave!

Dora drops the brooch into her purse and rushes to the tunnel door, slamming it shut and closing the latch. She's hustling for the front door of the shop when it hits her that this surfer is just what she needs. When Robert questions her about the stolen brooch, she'll tell him about the surfer who came up through the tunnel at closing time. She'll describe the surfer in precise detail. He'll be her perfect alibi!

She turns around and hurries to the back of the shop in time to hear a scratching sound on the other side of the tunnel door. The surfer is trying to get in, probably freezing his ass off. She lifts the latch for him and the door swings open.

It takes a moment for Dora to realize who is standing before her, clad in a shiny black wet suit and holding a long, sharp knife.

"Craig?"

She can't figure out what he's doing in the tunnel, but she sees quite clearly that one of his red-faced rages is coming on. She tries to shut the door but Craig pushes past her like a linebacker. To Dora's horror, he goes directly to the safe. He opens the safe door—*damn! it's still ajar!*—and looks inside. When he turns back to her, his face is a violent shade of crimson.

"Where'd you put it?"

Dora's neck begins to sweat.

"Where'd I put what?"

"You lying cow!" The back of his hand strikes her full force, and Dora falls backward through the tunnel door. Frantically, she grabs for a hold on the stair railing as Craig lunges at her, arm raised.

The blade plunges beneath her collarbone so swiftly that Dora feels nothing but the strange sensation of her legs giving out. She tumbles down the first few stairs, white stars slipping like iridescent raindrops through her vision. Motion stops and unbearable pain radiates through her chest. She's paralyzed, wedged between the damp cave wall and the stairs. The door is closing above her, and through the black tunnel Dora sees the light from the shop getting smaller and smaller. A memory flashes through her brain: a man in a white suit tugging at her sleeve, staring at her with piercing gray eyes. In the moment before she dies, Dora finally understands what he was trying to tell her:

You mustn't open that door.

A three-time Agatha nominee for his short stories, and guest of honor at Malice Domestic VIII, Peter Lovesey received the 2000 Diamond Dagger from the British Crime Writers Association for his distinguished mystery achievements, which include the Victorian-era series featuring Sergeant Cribb, books with modern-day detective Peter Diamond, and novels starring hapless sleuth Albert Edward "Bertie" Windsor, Prince of Wales. In this story, the villagers wonder why the elderly Miss Jackson would want to buy a cottage so far from the village—and why is she digging in the woods?

Away with the Fairies

Peter Lovesey

"Location, location, location" is supposed to be the mantra of home buyers. If so Miss Jackson hadn't heard of it. The cottage was not practical for a lady in her seventies who knew nobody. It stood a good half mile outside the village, in a clearing in the woods with access along a track that would test the suspension of any car. Picturesque, admittedly. Over the years, a succession of people had been tempted into ownership, but few had lasted more than a couple of years, and there had been some long spells when it was empty and up for sale. The estate agents danced on their desks after the old lady walked into their office and said she wanted the place because she'd lived there as a little girl.

May 30, 1938

I HATE it here. Hate the spiders and all the creepies. Hate the cottage and the smell of the oil lamps and the candles and the dark corners of the rooms. Hate the ugly pig called Tim and hate Mummy for marrying him.

She moved in one August afternoon and soon there were new lace curtains at the windows and a small yellow Citroen Special outside. People walking their dogs past the cottage caught glimpses of a short, wiry woman with permed silver hair. Her long-haired white cat was always on view, eyeing the dogs indifferently from an upstairs window.

A few elderly villagers remembered Bryony Jackson from before the war. They spoke of her with reserve, and it was evident that none of them planned to visit and talk about old times. Although she'd attended the village school, she had never been accepted as local. She wasn't from a village family. Her people, like so many previous owners of the cottage, had been suburban Londoners beguiled by the idea of a thatched home in the woods. They moved in, realized their mistake, and left after a year or so. They weren't even Wiltshire folk.

This was before the electricity was laid on and the bathroom was installed, so they must have found the conditions difficult. The parents had used bikes to get their shopping, and the child had walked through the woods to school. Nobody thought anything of it at the time.

"She were strange," Mrs. Maizey, mother of the shopkeeper, recalled. "You couldn't get friends with her if you tried. She weren't exactly stuck-up, just didn't want to join in things, so we let her be. There wasn't bullying as I recall. Nothing worse than pulling of her pigtails that all of us girls had to put up with."

June 10, 1938

Miss Stirling says I have to join in their stupid games, but I can't understand their silly singing, and they only laugh when I try, so why should I? This school is horrid. Children of all ages are in the same class and some of them have itchy things in their hair and don't bring hankies and some don't even wear shoes. I can't wait for the summer holiday. But then what will I do? Spend more time with Mummy and HIM? No thank you!!!

After a month or so, when she must have been busy sorting out the house, Miss Jackson started taking walks through the woods. The narrow footpaths ensured that if she met someone, she or they would have to step aside. She made it clear from the brisk way she thanked people and moved on that she wasn't interested in lingering to talk. Nobody was getting much out of her. If Thomas the postman couldn't persuade her to open up, no one would. She did her shopping at a supermarket in Devizes rather than the village shop. Admittedly, the local vegetables couldn't compare with what Safeway offered, but everyone suspected she still wouldn't have used the village even if everything was fresh each day.

It was interesting how Miss Jackson's determination to stay aloof only encouraged the locals to find out more. She was spotted buying a garden spade in Devizes, and the entire village discussed it. What would an old biddy be wanting with a spade when she had no garden? The ground around the cottage was simply the coarse turf that had been there for centuries. Surely she wasn't going to give herself extra work by cultivating it?

One morning as early as seven A.M., Thomas the postman saw the new spade resting against the wall of the cottage. There was fresh mud on the blade, indicating that Miss Jackson had left it out. Fair enough. She'd bought the thing, so she must have had a use for it. No, what intrigued Thomas (and everyone he told) was that there was no sign of digging in the vicinity of the cottage.

July 26, 1938

The holidays are here at last and hooray, I have found a secret place where I am writing this. I'll come here whenever I can and lie in a sunbeam, listening to the water trickle over the stones. It's a nice sound, like the fairies talking. I take off my sandals and socks and dip my feet in the cool stream. There are bright red toadstools and I found some lovely stripy feathers, blue, white, and black, that I'm using to decorate my magic place. I'm happy here.

"She could be digging up plants," suggested the younger Mrs. Maizey. "Folk do, and it's illegal now. Primroses and things are protected."

"Why would she dig up plants?"

"To sell 'em. Townspeople pay good money for a primrose."

"Violets," said the older Mrs. Maizey.

"Wild orchids," said the younger.

"Where would she keep 'em?" Thomas the postman asked.

"In the spare bedroom. She's got plenty of room in that cottage."

Most of the village had been inside Glade Cottage at some time in their lives, through knowing the owners, or through a window at the back in years when the place stood empty.

"That's daft," said Thomas. "Plants wouldn't survive indoors. Besides, how would she get 'em to a plantsman in that poky French car of hers?"

"All right, clever clogs. What's your theory?"

"I don't think it's plants," said Thomas. "I think something is buried in the woods."

"Something valuable?"

"Something she's dead keen to find, if it's worth buying a spade for. She knows a thing or two the rest of us don't. That's for sure."

"What would Bryony Jackson know? She hasn't lived here for the past sixty years."

"You'll have to ask her, won't you?"

"Are you thinking she saw something when she was a child?"

The senior Mrs. Maizey chuckled and wheezed. "Don't you know what she saw?"

Thomas the postman shook his head. "Before my time."

The young Mrs. Maizey said, "Tell him, Mother."

Old Mrs. Maizey was pink-faced. "Do you ever eat a boiled egg, postman?"

" 'Course I do."

"And after you scoop it out from the shell, do you poke your spoon through the bottom?"

"I do."

"And why? Do you know why?"

"Couldn't say. We've always done it in our family."

The old lady nodded. "Ours, too. 'Tis country lore. If you leave an eggshell unbroken there's a danger the little folk will take it away and put wheels on it and turn it into a coach."

"The fairies?" said Thomas with a wide smile.

She drew a sharp, disapproving breath. "You said it. In our family we never use the word."

"They're said to make all kinds of mischief," the younger Mrs. Maizey explained, "like snatching babies from their cradles and putting changelings in their place. I don't believe a word of it myself."

"Load of rot," Thomas confirmed.

Old Mrs. Maizey smiled wickedly. "Well, them's what Bryony Jackson saw. She said she saw them regular. She swore blind and it was in all the papers."

August 1, 1938

I was in my secret place all afternoon watching the pretty dragonfly things with blue wings that hover over the stream and I missed tea and got back when they were listening to the news on the wireless. Mummy was very cross and I wouldn't tell them where I had been. She said my clothes were in a dreadful state. I was sent to bed early and the pig sucked on his smelly horrible pipe and smiled.

The mystery of Miss Jackson and her digging continued to intrigue the locals. Those who hadn't been around in 1938 were treated to vivid accounts of the fairy sightings from Mrs. Maizey, old Ben Harmer, Olwen Sparrow, Walter Williams, and other veterans—in fact, from everyone except Bryony Jackson herself. Even if she had been on speaking terms with the villagers, it was too embarrassing a matter to raise with her. The memories varied as to detail, but the essentials were pretty well agreed upon. Sometime in the summer holidays of 1938, Bryony's solemn little face was on the front page of the local paper over a report that she had often seen and spoken to fairies in the woods where she lived. No one would have believed the child except that her stepfather, Timothy Walkinshaw, claimed to have seen one of them himself and had signed an affidavit that was reproduced in the *Observer* and the other national papers when they took up the story from the local press.

Bryony became a celebrity. She took a photographer from the *Daily Mirror* to get a picture of the fairies. He thought he saw something, but somehow the camera didn't capture it.

August 3, 1938

Yesterday as a punishment for spending so long in the woods and getting my clothes in a mess I was kept in all day, and today I was not allowed out of sight of the cottage. The pig was watching me from the window while I made a long daisy chain. I know he was hoping he could tell on me and get me into worse trouble. Mummy said she would smack my bottom if I disobeyed her, and I'm sure he wanted it to happen so he could be there to watch. So I did just as I was told, all day long. It was a boring, horrid day, but at least the pig was bored too and didn't get what he was hoping for, ha ha. Anyway, when Mummy smacks me she always makes sure he isn't about. He isn't even allowed to see me in the bath.

The new theory about Miss Jackson originated with someone other than the Maizeys—probably Olwen Sparrow, who had a morbid turn of mind. She was old enough to have been at school with Bryony. The theory was that shortly before the family left Glade Cottage in 1940, or thereabouts, Bryony got pregnant. Of course, it would have been a great scandal. Abortions were illegal, and (according to Olwen) Bryony kept the pregnancy a secret for a long time. Finally a baby was born. It didn't survive. Bryony's mother—who was known to be narrow-minded, even by the standards of the time—was said to have buried it secretly in the woods.

Olwen—in outlining this theory—was extremely vague. She didn't know for sure if the pregnancy had been true. She just thought she'd heard her parents discussing it. She would only hint that Bryony had murdered the child.

No one else remembered Bryony being pregnant, but then the war was on, and there was so much else to occupy everyone's attention. Mrs. Maizey senior said she thought the child had been too young to bear a child. But others thought it possible. The idea that she had returned after all these years to dig up her dead baby had a certain poignancy. Maybe her conscience had given her no peace and she wanted to give the child a proper burial. Maybe she would persuade the vicar to find a place for it in the churchyard.

"When does she do this digging?" Olwen's son Derek asked.

"At first light, before anyone is up," said Mrs. Maizey.

"I'm up," said Derek. "I'm an early riser. Happen I might take a walk through the woods tomorrow."

August 3, 1938

Another day making daisy chains. Mummy says if I promise to keep my clothes clean and be back by teatime I can play in the woods tomorrow. I know what will happen. I saw her look at the pig when she was talking to me and he winked at her. She wants him to spy on me. When we were having dinner, he asked me what games I play in the woods. I told him I don't play games. I said I visit the fairies. He told me it's wicked to make things up and I said I wasn't making anything up. There really were fairies in the woods and they were my friends. He says he doesn't believe me, but I think he does, a little bit. Well, I say let him try and spy on me because I have a SECRET PLAN.

Derek Sparrow got up before five and was waiting within view of Glade Cottage and listening to the dawn chorus and wondering if he was on a fool's errand when Miss Jackson came out wearing green Wellingtons and carrying her spade. She headed off purposefully down one of the footpaths between the bracken. When it was safe to follow, Derek took the same route.

August 4, 1938

Mummy left early to go shopping and I went out soon after. The pig was wearing boots and gaiters and had his field glasses on the table, so I knew he was going to try and follow me. I could easily have run on and lost him, only I didn't. I walked to another part of the woods a long way from my magic place. When I got to a fallen tree I sat down and pretended to hide something in a hole in the trunk. I knew he was not far off, watching me with the glasses, because I saw the sun flash on them. In a minute I pretended to move on, but really I hid behind some bushes and got ready. Just as I thought, nosy Pig came to look in the hollow. AND WHAT A SURPRISE HE GOT!

Derek could hear the sound of digging ahead, so he approached stealthily, using the trees as cover. Presently he caught sight of the old lady at a lower level where a stream coursed downward among stones. Evidently she had been working here before, because a large heap of scrub lay to one side. She had cleared an area of about three square meters at the side of the stream and was now scraping the surface with the spade, shifting stones and roots. It looked hard work for someone of her age.

Once, she stopped and leaned on the spade and sighed so loudly that he heard her from where he was. Then she turned and looked straight in his direction, just as if *he* had sighed. He ducked and kept very still and she went back to the work.

After half an hour it was obvious that she was digging deeper, taking divots from one small area. It was slow progress; she had to rest every few minutes. Derek could have shifted the earth in half the time. He kept thinking she could bring on a heart attack doing heavy work at her age. He was getting sorry for her.

At the depth of little more than the spade length the edge of the blade struck something metal. The sound was unmistakable. She put down the spade and knelt beside the hole and shifted some earth with her hands.

Derek crept toward a bramble just large enough to shelter behind.

Miss Jackson picked up the spade and tried to lever something out. She wasn't much good at it. All she got was a metallic scraping sound. After a number of tries she flung down the spade and said, "Oh, God help me!"

By now Derek's admiration for the old lady's efforts had reached a point where he felt compelled to respond. He couldn't bear to watch her pathetic efforts any longer. So he played God. Standing up, he stepped down the bank toward her and said, "Morning, Miss Jackson."

She stared at him open-mouthed.

"Can I help?" he asked.

She shook her head and took a step back from the hole.

"What have you got here?" Derek asked. "Buried treasure?"

"What are you doing here?"

He said something about early morning walks. He crouched by the hole and looked into it. "It looks like a tin box of some sort."

Miss Jackson had snatched up the spade and lifted it to shoulder height, threatening him. "Get away from there! It's mine."

He backed off, trying to calm her. "Easy. I'm only trying to help. I'm Derek—Mrs. Sparrow's son."

"Olwen Sparrow?" She lowered the spade a little.

"You remember?"

"Some things, yes."

"Mother was at school with you. I happened to see you here and thought you were in trouble."

"It's just something I buried a long time ago."

"Want me to get it out?"

She sighed, lowered the spade, and gave a nod.

To Derek's eye, the box appeared too small to hold a dead baby. It was coffin-shaped, certainly, narrow and oblong, but it was only about nine inches long. He flicked away some dirt and saw the words "Sharp's Toffees" on the lid.

"What's inside?"

"Memories," she said.

He used a sharp-edged stone to force out enough earth to get his fingers underneath. Then he lifted it from the hole. It felt light in weight, but there was definitely something inside.

Miss Jackson grabbed it from him and held it to her chest.

"Aren't you going to open it?"

"Not here. Would you pass me the spade?"

"I'd better carry it for you, if you're going to hang on to the tin." She was gripping that box in a way that left no doubt she would not let go of it.

They walked together through the woods toward her cottage. Derek asked, "What was it like, growing up here during the war?"

"Before the war," she said. "We came before the war."

"And lived in Glade Cottage?"

"Yes."

"Just you and your mum and dad?"

"He wasn't my father. My father died in London when I was quite small."

"How long were you here?"

"Two or three years. They parted—my mother and stepfather—and we went back to Wimbledon, Mother and me."

Derek got nothing more from Miss Jackson. At the cottage door she could have invited him in for a coffee after the good turn he'd done, but she didn't.

He said, "I'd like to know what we dug up."

She said, "It's private."

August 5, 1938

I never thought I would feel sorry for the pig, and I don't. But I almost do. Mummy didn't believe him when he said he'd seen a fairy in the woods. She likes people to tell the truth, however bad it is. He was scared to say he'd seen me undressed, because that's rude and Mummy's really modest and it would have made her very upset and angry, so he told her what I made him say—that it must have been a fairy he saw. Mummy laughed at first and asked what this fairy looked like and I butted in and said it was quite big and wasn't wearing any clothes and he had to agree. Mummy frowned then and got cross when he kept saying it really happened. In the end, she said he would never get her to believe it, and he said would she believe him if it was in the paper? So a lady from the paper came this afternoon and talked to us about the fairy. I said I'd seen fairies lots of times in the woods and the pig said he'd seen this one yesterday at a place where I took him. Now they want to try and get a photograph for the paper.

August 8, 1938

It was in the paper, all about the fairy. No picture, of course, but there's a picture of me with Tim the pig. He looks so uncomfortable, just like he's sitting on a hedgehog. Now more papers want to come and talk to us this afternoon. It's very funny. And the funniest thing of all is that Mummy STILL doesn't believe a word of it. But she isn't cross with me. She thinks the pig must have made me say it, about the fairy. They are having HUGE arguments.

Alone in the cottage, Bryony Jackson lifted the lid from the tin and took out an object wrapped in oilskin cloth. It was her diary of 1938. For some time she had been reading in the papers about recovered memories—people who had gone to counselors and psychiatrists and discovered dark truths they had suppressed all their adult lives. She wanted to know if her stepfather, Tim, had abused her as a child. Else why had the marriage ended so abruptly with his quitting the house in 1938? You heard so much about wicked things happening to children. It had begun to worry her after she heard about women recovering childhood memories, and the worry had increased until it almost reached the level of mental torment. But she would never go to a psychiatrist. Anyway, there were counterclaims about something called false memory syndrome.

The childish handwriting was still legible. She spent the next hour totally absorbed, thankful for the chance to unlock her past in privacy, reassured when she was certain no sexual abuse had taken place, but appalled to learn how manipulative a jealous child can be.

August 10, 1938

The pig left us this morning. Mummy says he's gone to live somewhere else. She asked me lots of questions about what happened in the woods and if I had anything I wanted to tell her. Of course there was nothing. Nothing happened except me giving him the fright of his life by coming from behind a tree in my birthday suit, but I can't tell her that now, can I? Tim the pig didn't dare tell Mummy he'd seen me like that. She would have thought it was his fault for sure. She hates rude people, specially rude men. She's always warning me about nasty men. So he had to tell her what I told him to say. Seeing a fairy might have sounded silly to a grown-up, but it wasn't rude or nasty, because fairies don't wear clothes usually. Mummy says she and I won't have to live here much longer. She doesn't like the place anymore. That's a pity, in a way. I think I could get to like it now.

Margaret Maron's two mystery series feature self-possessed police lieutenant Sigrid Harald and North Carolina judge Deborah Knott. Knott has appeared in nine works, including Maron's Edgar-, Agatha-, Anthony-, and Macavity-winning novel Bootlegger's Daughter *and her Agatha Award-winning story "Deborah's Judgement." Her most recent Knott books are* Storm Track *and* Common Clay. *In this story, Maron looks at a long-held secret which still echoes for the family involved . . .*

The Choice

Margaret Maron

"Kate?"

She whirled around, the blood draining from her face, then returning so rapidly that she flushed like an embarrassed schoolgirl.

"I'm sorry," Sam said. "I didn't mean to startle you. I thought you heard me when I came in."

He peered over his wife's slender shoulder through the tall narrow window slit that gave light to the stair landing and realized suddenly that this was not the first time he'd found her here.

"What do you see out there?" he asked.

He himself saw nothing except bright sunlight playing on an overgrown pasture that sloped down to a creek. He couldn't even see the creek for it was hidden by the trees and underbrush that grew thickly along its sandy banks. They had talked about horses when they first moved here, when the children were little, and they'd had a few chickens and, briefly, some goats to eat out the poison ivy and stinging nettles. The youngest child was in college now, and their only animals were a couple of dogs and some stray cats that nobody had the heart to take to the pound. Small pine trees were starting to spring up in the pasture.

Although they'd both grown up on working farms—or maybe it was more accurate to say that because they'd both grown up *working* on farms right here in eastern North Carolina—they had no romantic illusions about getting back to the earth. Tobacco was already loosening its stranglehold on the area, and even if it weren't, neither Sam nor Kate had any desire to spend their lives in such hot, sweaty, dirty work. No, when they came back to the country, it was on *their* terms, with college degrees that allowed them to work in Raleigh yet still raise their children in a loving community of aunts and uncles and grandparents, on a ten-acre piece of land where there was space for the children to run and play freely, safely.

"What are you looking at?" he asked again. His chin brushed her soft brown hair, hair that was gently going gray, like the first random flakes of snow falling on autumn leaves.

"Nothing," she said, leaning back against his chest in the familiar circle of his arms. "Not a thing." Yet she continued to gaze out the window, so he did, too.

And then, of course, he saw it. Odd that he'd never noticed before. By some trick of architecture, this was the only window in the house that was high enough to overlook the trees along the creek bottom to where the land rose beyond. Near the top of the rise was a ruined chimney, two stories tall, a visible reminder of the house that once stood there.

"Do you ever feel time fold back against itself?" she asked him. "Sometimes I stand here and can almost see the house the way it used to look with Tim and me racing down the hill with our fishing poles, heading for the creek after a day in the fields. As if those two little kids were the reality and I was a ghost out of their future."

"The future doesn't have ghosts."

"Doesn't it? Remember when we were building this house? I stood right here—it was the same day they put the roof trusses on—and you and the children were outside picking up nails where the driveway was going to go. I remember thinking to myself that I'd grow old in this house and I would stand at this very window and watch a grown-up child come up from the creek. It felt so real, I could almost see it. Last weekend, when Chris was out here—" Her voice trembled and broke off.

He turned her in his arms and looked down into her troubled face. "Kate, the kids are back and forth all the time. Of course they're going to go down to the creek. They used to spend half their lives splashing around down there. There's nothing odd about seeing Chris through this or any other window."

"No? Then why did I have the exact same feeling I had twenty years ago? As if I ought to be able to look up and see the sky through the trusses."

"Déjà vu all over again?" he teased. Then, as he felt her shoulders tighten, he added sympathetically, "You've been working too hard. And all this strain with your mother. You were out there this afternoon, weren't you?"

She nodded. "It's not that, though. She's adjusting to the place very nicely. Likes the food, likes the staff, likes her room."

"What, then?"

A small shrug of her shoulders. "The aide was changing the sheets when I got there, and Mama was up in her wheelchair. The aide said something about her cold feet, and Mama said that was one of the things she missed the most after her husband died. Not having somebody there beside her that she could warm her cold feet on."

"And?" he asked in puzzlement.

Even though his family had known the Cole family when they were children, they were in different school districts and hadn't met till high school. Like the rest of the community, he'd heard of the tragedy, though—how Mr. Cole had fallen asleep with a lighted cigarette after being up half the night with his wife when she miscarried their third child, how Kate and her older brother Tim blamed themselves because they might have noticed the fire in time to raise the alarm if they hadn't skipped their chores and gone fishing.

Not that Kate ever talked much about it, or about their father, either, for that matter. Even after they were married, it was years before she confided that her father had been drinking that day. In that time, in that churchly community, excessive drinking—drunkenness—had been a shameful secret that every affected family tried to keep hidden. She chattered freely of the poor but loving grandparents who took them in, the aunts and uncles who'd helped out. Only rarely did she speak of her father, and never about his death. When Tim reminisced about the water wheels Mr. Cole built for him on the creek bank or the times they went hunting together, Kate would somehow drift away to the kitchen to make coffee or fill a glass or check on the kids.

It was years before Sam actually noticed, and when he did, he put it down to the pain and embarrassment she must still feel.

Mrs. Cole was a different matter. A sickly woman who shied from any sort of confrontation, she had bravely borne her widowhood, devoting herself to the welfare of her two children. Her two *fatherless* children. She had a way of reminding you of how she had sacrificed her health to make up to them for their loss. And hers, too, of course. A hot-tempered man, folks said, but a good man and a hard worker. Made the children work hard, too, they said. Hard work never hurt anybody, and just look how fine those children turned out, both of them teachers, both of them upright pillars of the community.

"After all these years, don't you think it's sort of sweet that she still misses him?"

"Daddy's been dead almost thirty-five years," Kate said. "And she quit sleeping in his bed long before that."

That surprised him. "But I thought she was in the hospital with a miscarriage."

"Even a poor marriage can still have sex," Kate said dryly as she turned back to the window.

But somebody to warm her cold feet on? Kate wondered what would Mama say if suddenly reminded of the way she flinched whenever he grabbed her breast in front of them and pulled her up the rickety stairs to his bedroom and slammed the door, leaving her and Tim to pretend nothing unpleasant was happening up there? Not that she had really understood, but Tim was two years older and he certainly had. That must have been why he always tried to distract her during those bad times. Protecting her emotions. Unable to protect his own. She shuddered to think of the lasting damage to his emotional psyche if their father hadn't died when he did. So why should it bother her if Tim had managed to bury the pain and angry humiliation of their childhood, if Mama pretended her marriage had been as warm and loving as Sam and hers?

Most of the time, she didn't care, just let her mind go blank. But today, standing at this window, staring across to the ruined house of her childhood, Kate wondered if she were the only one who remembered how things really were . . .

They were tenant farmers. Sharecroppers. Unlanded gentry.

Maybe that was the acid that ate at him and corroded his soul. Moving from farm to farm every few years. Living in tiny little shacks or huge dilapidated houses like this one, with no indoor plumbing, as though it were the 1870s, not the 1970s. Knowing that the labor of his body and that of his wife and children would never earn enough to buy back the land that his own father had gambled away in the forties. Or maybe it was just the alcohol. Rotgut whiskey or a case of Bud when he had a few dollars. Fermented tomato juice or aftershave lotion when he didn't.

Not that he was drunk all the time. That's what made it so horrible. The unpredictability of his rages. He could go months without a drop, months where, when the fieldwork was done for the day, he'd help little Katie plant flower seeds or whittle slingshots, and yes, water wheels for Timmy. Then, for no reason they could ever fathom, he'd go roaring off to town and come home in a black drunken rage that could last for days. Near the end, those rages seemed to come more often and with more violence.

Like the day he'd carried Mama to the hospital because she was bleeding so badly. Katie and Timmy were scared and wanted to go with them, but he'd ordered them out to the field.

"And I'd better see every one of them tobacco plants suckered by the time I get back," he'd told them.

All morning they'd toiled up and down the rows of sticky green plants, snapping off the suckers that tried to grow up where the money leaves met the plant's stem. At lunchtime they stopped just long enough for sandwiches and glasses of cold milk before heading back into the broiling field with only their wide-brimmed straw hats for shade. Feet bare on the hot dirt, their bare arms and legs burned brown by the sun.

An hour later Timmy had gone back to the house for a jug of water, and that's where he was when their father came home and accused him of slacking off while his little sister was out there working as she'd been told.

Katie heard his screams from the edge of the field, but experience had taught her there was nothing she could do except blank her mind and keep on snapping the suckers.

When Timmy took his place beside her in the next row, his legs were red and raw. The welts from the belt marched up and down her brother's backside like rows of newly seeded corn.

"Did Mama come home?" she whispered. Not that Mama had ever been able to step between Timmy and the belt.

Timmy shook his head and kept moving.

They finished the field a little before four. Timmy didn't want to go back to the house, but Katie was bolder. Their father almost never hit her. Just Timmy and Mama. "Besides, I'll bet he's passed out on the bed by now."

That was something else experience had taught her.

But even though he was two years older, Timmy couldn't be persuaded. Instead he fetched a hoe and headed for the vegetable garden. "He said for us to start chopping grass if we got done early."

She slipped into the old wooden house quieter than the mice usually were. Silence was all around. At the foot of the staircase she hesitated until she heard deep snores from above. Relief flowed down like healing waters on her sore heart then, and she tiptoed up the stairs, the stairs he'd knocked Mama down this morning, though he said it was an accident when he saw all the blood.

His bedroom was at the top of the stairs, and as her eyes got level with the landing, Katie could see him sprawled on his back, his head on the pillow, loud ragged snores issuing from his open mouth. She tiptoed closer. The sheet had come untucked and there was a cigarette-shaped scorch mark on the cotton mattress ticking. At least this time he'd put his cigarette in the ashtray on the nightstand. It had burned right down to the filter, leaving an acrid smell in the room. There were more little scorch marks all around on the bare wood floor where cigarettes had dropped from his fingers when he fell asleep. Last winter he'd actually burned his chest and fingers when he passed out with a freshly lit one. Mama kept saying they'd all be burned alive in their beds some night.

She thought of Timmy's raw legs, of Mama's bloody dress and the way she'd held her swollen belly and moaned as she hobbled to the car.

Timmy's legs.

Mama's blood.

"It's okay," she told Timmy, whose eyes were almost as red as the welts on his legs from crying. "He's drunk as a skunk and won't remember how much chopping needed doing today. Let's you and me go fishing, okay? Catch us a few sun perch for supper."

She pulled a couple of long cane poles from the shed and sidetracked Timmy when he headed for the compost pile with a small shovel to dig for worms. "Wait and dig 'em out of the creek bank," she said. "It'll be cooler there."

As they hurried along the path that would lead them

through the thick underbrush down to the creek, Katie paused and looked back.

A tendril of gray smoke leaked from the upstairs bedroom window.

Abruptly, like a startled doe who feels the hunter's eye upon her, she whirled around and searched with her own eyes the pasture that rose on the other side of the creek, an empty pasture where no house was yet built.

No one was there, though. No one had watched her before and no one cried out in alarm now.

No one.

"So your mother sees their marriage through rose-colored glasses," said Sam. "After thirty-five years, let the old woman rewrite her past if it makes her happy. Haven't you ever wanted to?"

Kate stood so long without answering that Sam tightened his arms around her. "Hey, it was just a rhetorical question. It's not as if you really have a choice."

No choice? When out there, across the creek, she could almost see the ten-year-old child she'd once been looking straight at her? If she leaned forward, rapped on the window, would the child turn? Run back up to the house? Raise the alarm?

"Of course not," she told Sam. "And even if I could rewrite the past, I wouldn't."

"C'mon, Katie!" Timmy called impatiently. "Whatcha looking at?"

"Nothing," Katie said. "Not a thing." And ran down through the underbrush to join her brother.

Baltimore resident Sujata Massey received an Agatha Award for her first novel, The Salaryman's Wife, *featuring antiques dealer Rei Shimura, who also appears in* Zen Attitude, *the Agatha-nominated* The Flower Master, *and* The Floating Girl. *In this story, Rei investigates the life of a persecuted teenager in Japan.*

Junior High Samurai

Sujata Massey

The samurai held a long, curved sword over the peasant prostrate on the ground before him. From the veranda of a nearby teahouse, noblemen and a courtesan had abandoned their tea drinking to gawk.

"So, what makes better afternoon entertainment: murder or a cup of tea?" I asked my class of Japanese fourteen-year-olds, some of whom were blatantly sleeping on their desks.

I'd hoped that a color slide of a murder would make the snoozing students open their eyes. I'd guessed wrong. Teaching is not what I do best. My name is Rei Shimura; I am based in Tokyo, where I sell Japanese antiques. The story I'm going to tell you happened during the worst of the Japanese economic downturn—the year my clientele held so tightly to its yen that I had to moonlight as an art history teacher at Makigahara Junior High.

"This scene from the famous play *The Loyal League of Forty-seven Ronin* has been illustrated by dozens of artists over the years. The Hokusai print was one of the earliest. What's interesting about this picture?" I said, using my pen to tap the color slide I was projecting.

I glanced at Hiroki Kogi, the slim, fine-featured boy who sat between Akira Kimura and Yukio Kondo in the fourth row. Hiroki was straining to make out details in the slide. He used to wear bottle-thick glasses, but he'd stopped, perhaps because of the teasing from his classmates.

"Come on, everyone," I cajoled. "We've been discussing how woodblock print artists were photographers of their time, capturing ordinary people and landscapes. But this isn't ordinary—why do you think it caught Hokusai's interest?"

Yukio, who I'd thought was just a dumb jock, surprised me by raising his hand. "Hokusai must have been ordered to do it, just like we're ordered to do things in school."

Not exactly, but I could stretch his point to suit the day's topic. I said, "Remember that before the 1860s there was no national school system. Theatrical plays, and artwork retelling the plays, were ways to teach people the values considered part of the cultural identity."

The end-of-class bell rang. As the girls wearing sailor blouses and pleated skirts and boys in high-necked black uniforms bowed and began filing out, Yukio and Akira yanked Hiroki Kogi's collar. Hiroki winced but didn't turn around or do anything to complain.

During my lunch break I joined two other teachers, Miss

Ito and Mrs. Nakagawa, at a table near the school's athletic field.

"I can't understand some of the kids in my class—Yukio Kondo and Akira Kimura, especially. They're so brutal to Hiroki Kogi," I said, munching on a sweet tofu pocket stuffed with rice that Miss Ito had brought to share. The lunches were a nice way for me to enjoy home-cooked Japanese food and learn a little more about Miss Ito, who taught science, and Mrs. Nakagawa, who taught Japanese.

"Other schools have worse bullies," Miss Ito said. "In Tokyo, some schoolgirls set another girl on fire because they didn't like her socks!"

"I don't think the boys you mentioned are brutal," Mrs. Nakagawa commented. "They can't help noticing what's different. Hiroki Kogi used to wear thick glasses. He's got contact lenses now, so things must be better. Anyway, he's a good student. He scored perfectly the last *kanji* examination."

"He doesn't wear contacts—I'm sure because of the way he squints and bumps into things," I said. "He does well in my class because he studies art books from the library." At that moment, Hiroki was seated under a persimmon tree, reading a book. He was so engrossed that he didn't see Yukio and Akira approaching him. Yukio kicked the book out of Hiroki's lap. He clutched his hand, while his face seemed to crumple in pain.

"Did you see that? We've got to do something!" I stood up.

"No, no! You shouldn't interfere," Mrs. Nakagawa said earnestly, and Miss Ito nodded.

"Why not?"

"You are a part-time teacher in an elective subject, Miss Shimura," Miss Ito reminded me. "Don't worry about the children so much. You have another life outside this school. Relax and enjoy it and your big, beautiful apartment in Tokyo."

"My place is really nothing special," I said, feeling flustered by the acidity in Miss Ito's voice. I'd invited her once for dinner, but she left after a half hour, saying that she had to get home to take care of her mother. Something about my place must have repelled her—or was it my overgrilled eggplant?

I turned my attention back to the students. Yukio and Akira were still in front of Hiroki, who had shrunk like a turtle retreating into his shell. Hiroki reached into his pocket and handed something to Akira. Akira's laugh was harsh enough to carry over to us. He and Yukio strolled off, throwing a baseball to each other.

"It looks as if Hiroki paid money to Akira!" I was getting more outraged by the minute.

"One can't be certain," Miss Ito commented. "Here, eat some more *inarizushi*."

"I need to know what happened." I strode off, not wanting to hear any more words of caution.

When I was close enough for Hiroki to recognize me, he brushed his face with his hand. The dirt streaked across his cheek, so it was evident that he had tears in his eyes.

"What happened between you and those boys?"

"Nothing! I was just reading," he answered quickly.

"I saw them take something from you. It was money, wasn't it?"

"No," he answered, avoiding my eyes.

"I saw you give something to them, just as I saw them come up and kick the book out of your lap."

"Miss Shimura, am I in trouble with you?" Hiroki's voice quavered.

"No! I'm sorry about what happened. Do you want to sit near me, just to be on the safe side?"

He shook his head violently. "I couldn't! Everyone would say I was a baby."

"Well, maybe you should sit near some other students?" I suggested gently.

"They don't want me."

As he spoke, a memory flashed back from my own past life in California, during the time that I transferred from a diverse urban high school to a predominantly white private school. During the first month at the new school, there was no room for me at any lunch table, and for the first time I heard the word "gook."

Hiroki was a Japanese student at an all-Japanese school, but he was suffering the same problems. As Mrs. Nakagawa had said, something about Hiroki made it difficult for him to fit in with the others. Extreme near-sightedness didn't seem enough of a reason for anyone to make a child's life a living hell.

The following day I noticed that Hiroki Kogi's right hand was tightly wrapped in a white bandage.

"It's a sprain," Hiroki said when I asked him about it after class. "It hardly hurts anymore, but I'm afraid my writing will be very poor."

"You don't have to write anything until it's better. I'll tell the other teachers about it."

"Oh, no, Miss Shimura. You are too kind to me because you are foreign. I'm afraid the other teachers expect me to do my homework and write exams and so on."

"I think I should talk to the principal, then."

"Please don't!" Hiroki whispered, looking around as if worried someone had heard me. "It will only become worse. They saw you talking to me at lunch yesterday, and they asked what I said. I told them that I said nothing, but I don't think they believe me. So please don't talk to me again."

At lunch I brought up what had happened with Mrs.

Nakagawa and Miss Ito. I had a bit of humble pie to eat, since Hiroki had told me essentially what the teachers had: that to interfere would only bring trouble.

"Do you think there are hidden social factors that cause Hiroki to be ostracized as well as bullied?" I asked after offering my homemade cucumber sushi rolls.

"It's probably the mother's fault," Mrs. Nakagawa said. "If a mother is too unusual or permissive, her child won't blend in with the others."

"Don't you think, though," Miss Ito said, laying down her chopsticks, "the problem might be because of his father?"

"How?" I asked, liking the way Miss Ito wasn't so quick to blame everything on women. Miss Ito was unusual for Japanese—never married, and she looked to be older than forty.

"Well, Hiroki's father has a high position at Makigahara Bank, so the family has a house that is probably better than others in the neighborhood. And I recall that Hiroki entered school one year ago, not two years ago like the others."

"They came late because the family was in America," Mrs. Nakagawa said. "His father took the family to New York for some time. Children who studied abroad are different. Not very Japanese."

"It seems unfair to be marked as different, just because of a little overseas experience," I said, thinking it amazing that Hiroki had never spoken to me in English, since everyone at school knew my background. "Maybe I can talk in class a little bit about how I was educated in America, but I have been able to work and live happily in Japan."

"The best way for a teacher to help is never to single anyone out for special attention," Mrs. Nakagawa said. "Treat the group well, and in turn the group will be happy and behave harmoniously with each other." She sounded like the school's teaching manual. "Miss Shimura, may I trouble you for some more *kappa-maki?* It's very tasty. It's practically impossible to tell that it was made by a foreigner!"

School was in session Saturday mornings, but as art history wasn't scheduled for that day, I had free time. I spent the morning and half the afternoon on my balcony refinishing a cedar *tansu* chest.

As I rubbed, I thought about how Makigahara Junior High was considered one of the best feeders to a top high school, which in turn fed students to Waseda University. The school seemed the wrong place for Hiroki. I wondered how much his parents knew about his suffering. I went inside and found my teaching folder, which contained Hiroki's telephone number and address, along with data on the other students. I dialed his number and heard the phone ringing endlessly. This was odd. Every Japanese person I knew had an answering machine.

Hiroki's home was a few blocks away from my aunt's address, so I knew I could find it. I'd stop in to say hello to his parents and find a way to bring up the bullying.

The Kogi house was built on a double lot, one of the largest single-family residences in their neighborhood. With its freshly painted white stucco walls and dark blue tiled roof, the house was extremely pretty, and quite typical of the residential style of architecture that flourished during the 1980s boom years of the bubble economy. I bet they'd built the house before they went off to the United States.

"Yes?" A woman's voice blared out of the intercom box a few seconds after I pushed the doorbell next to the house gate. It was six o'clock, so I thought everyone would likely be home.

"Kogi-sama?" I used the most polite form of address, assuming I was speaking to Hiroki's mother. "This is Rei Shimura, I teach your son art history—"

"Bad news travels fast," she said, and the intercom went dead.

Feeling confused, I watched a slender woman clatter out of the house, shoving her bare feet into rubber garden slippers as she came down the path to open the gate. Mrs. Kogi wore a tailored cotton blouse tucked into slim jeans, and her long hair was caught up in a ponytail. As youthful as Mrs. Kogi's appearance was, she moved as if she was in pain. When she got closer, I noticed her bloodshot eyes.

"I came to check your son's injury and to see if you wanted to know anything about what's going on at school," I began.

"Injury? You mean you found Hiroki? Oh, I must call my husband!" Mrs. Kogi ran back into the house.

I followed her, stepping out of my shoes and onto the polished wooden floor. "I'm afraid I don't know what you're talking about. Is Hiroki missing?"

"Yes. He never came home today." Mrs. Kogi stared at me. "I thought the school knew. I left a message on the office's answering machine. Isn't that why you're here?"

Before I could respond, a short, slender man wearing thick glasses came down the stairs. Mr. Kogi looked at me with an expression that seemed hostile. He didn't greet me, nor did he duck his head in a bow. Like his wife, he was casually dressed in jeans.

"This is Miss Shimura," Mrs. Kogi said. "She is Hiroki's teacher."

"I've been worried about Hiroki," I began. I described what had happened in the schoolyard.

Mrs. Kogi told me Hiroki hadn't said how he'd gotten hurt, but she'd taken him to the doctor for evaluation. Then, on the next evening—Friday—Hiroki came home late from school and rushed upstairs to his room, refusing the dinner his mother had made for him.

"When my wife told me about Hiroki's strange behavior, I wanted to speak to him," Mr. Kogi said. "My son did not want to unlock his door, but I insisted. Finally, when I went in, I saw his face. He had been abused."

"Oh, no!" I exclaimed. "When I saw him waiting to catch the bus on Friday, he looked fine. Something must have happened after school."

"The trouble began after Hiroki got off the bus," Mr. Kogi said. "He told me that two boys followed him and demanded that he buy them beer from an outdoor vending machine. It was bad luck that the neighborhood constable walked by and demanded to see Hiroki's identification card. Hiroki was frightened we would be angry, so he pointed to the bushes where the other two were hiding and said they were the ones who wanted beer, not him."

"He stood up for himself!" I said, amazed at his bravery.

"As soon as the policeman left, the two jumped my son," Mr. Kogi continued in a level tone. "The boys only stopped when some adults came walking down the street. Hiroki ran home. After we talked yesterday evening, I tried to reassure my son that everything would be all right, but I went to bed quite worried. I had thought Makigahara Junior High was the best possible place for him to study. Now I'm not sure."

"This morning, Hiroki was downstairs two hours earlier than usual," Mrs. Kogi said. "He told me that he was going to school early to avoid the bullies on the bus. When he said that, I felt worried about what might happen on the bus after school—and now my worries have come to haunt me."

"Did you call the police?"

"Yes. They say it is not an emergency because he has only been missing for six hours. They thought he might be coming home on a very late bus. But I know that won't happen. He must have been beaten again." Mrs. Kogi sounded desolate, and her husband looked at me as if he were embarrassed. Maybe he would have comforted his wife had I not been there. Japanese people don't like to touch in front of others.

"Did you mention to them about the ongoing harassment by Yukio Kondo and Akira Kimura?" I asked.

"Oh, are those their names? Hiroki wouldn't tell us. Already you have been a great help, Miss Shimura," Mrs. Kogi said, sniffling. "Yes, I told the police there was a problem with two boys at the beer vending machine the previous day, and they said something like 'boys will be boys.'"

"I'll try to think of places where he might have gone. How early may I call you tomorrow morning to check that Hiroki came back?" I tried to put things in a positive light.

Mrs. Kogi put her head in her hands. "Call us any time. I believe we will not sleep."

I didn't sleep much, either. At five A.M. I got up to study my class list. I had the phone numbers for Yukio's and Akira's families, but I didn't dare go to them directly as I had with the Kogi family. My visit to Hiroki Kogi's parents had been unsettling. There was something about them that didn't seem quite right. Mr. Kogi had been so calm, and Mrs. Kogi so upset. They were complete opposites. Part of me—a darker part—wondered if one of Hiroki's parents had something to do with his disappearance. Blaming it on bullies was a perfect excuse.

No, I decided. Mr. Kogi had seemed emotionless because that was how Japanese men were supposed to be. He probably felt as panicky as his wife.

I called the Kogis at eight o'clock. Hiroki was still missing.

"The police have been here and taken photographs to use in their search." Mrs. Kogi sounded exhausted. "Now it is out of our hands and into theirs."

Not quite. I ate a quick breakfast and packed my student directory in my backpack before boarding a train to Yokohama. Slumped in a half-empty compartment, I stared at the advertisements decorating the walls. Pretty Festival Wedding Hall could provide music, fake flowers, and a Chinese buffet to please the most discriminating mother. Work-up, a stimulant-spiked beverage, would keep you wired. Makigahara Bank, Mr. Kogi's employer, was offering home mortgage loans at a low interest rate, making it possible to buy a dream house. How ironic; the Kogis had their own dream house, but now its heart was missing.

When I reached Minami-Makigahara train station, I disembarked and telephoned Miss Ito. I wanted to ask what she thought I should do. Miss Ito was not home, her aged mother told me. Not giving myself time to doubt my action, I telephoned Akira Kimura's house. A pleasant woman's voice answered.

"Um, I wonder if Akira-san is home?" I said, pitching my voice a little higher and breathier.

"Who is calling, please?"

"Um, I'm calling from school," I said, hoping she'd assume I was just Akira's classmate.

"Well, then, don't you know it's baseball season? There's a home game today. Akira went to play."

That meant Yukio was there, too. I caught the bus that ran to Makigahara Junior High. This was the same bus line that ran past Hiroki's neighborhood. Before disembarking, I asked the bus driver if he knew a student named Hiroki Kogi.

"I pick up many schoolchildren each time I drive my route. I don't know them by name," he told me, keeping his eyes on the road.

"He's fourteen but very small, and wears thick glasses," I explained. "Or when he doesn't wear glasses, he bumps into things. Lately he's been wearing a bandage on his right hand."

"Ah, that one. He usually catches this bus to school, but he wasn't on my route Saturday. I didn't think much about it. Is he all right?"

"I hope so," I said. "There's a problem with bullies. Did you ever notice two tall boys harassing Hiroki?"

"Oh, yes, I know those two," the driver grunted. "They were on my bus yesterday, running a little late to school, if I remember correctly. Good-for-nothings."

I thanked the driver and got off at the school. Fifteen minutes before the game's start, the stands were filling with parents and children. I slipped onto the field and started for the home team dugout.

"It's Shimura-*sensei*."

"What's she doing here?"

The other boys on the team whispered among themselves as I strode by, searching for Yukio and Akira. If I remembered right, they were both on the team, but Akira had a more important position—first baseman—while Yukio was in the outfield. I hoped that I could speak to each of them separately.

Yukio was near the dugout, where he was practicing his batting moves. I watched him swing the bat through the air, thinking that a punch from him would flatten me. It could do even more damage to Hiroki, who was barely five feet tall.

"I want to talk to you," I said.

"*Sensei,* the game starts in a few minutes," Yukio whined. "The coach wouldn't let me."

"Does the coach know about what you and Akira did to Hiroki?" As Yukio's expression changed, I said, "Let's move away where we can speak privately."

"I want to stop bothering him," Yukio said when we had

gone off to the batting cage. "I want to stop, but I don't know how. Akira is the one who wants his money."

"Crazy enough to kill? What did the two of you do to Hiroki yesterday morning before school?"

"Nothing! I didn't see him before school because Akira and I got in late. I noticed that Hiroki wasn't in class."

"What did you do, beat him up and leave him somewhere?"

"No, I didn't see him! When he wasn't in school, I thought he might have been home in bed. I feel bad about it, Shimura-*sensei*. I won't do anything like that again."

"Where's Akira?" It struck me as odd that the two weren't practicing their swings together.

"He went inside the school. He's coming out now," Yukio said, pointing at a solidly built boy in a bright yellow uniform coming out of the school.

Without saying goodbye, I jogged off to catch Akira before he got swept up in the game crowd.

"Oh, um, Miss Shimura," Akira said when I blocked his path.

"What were you doing inside the building?" I asked.

"Taking a—I can't say the word, sorry. It's not polite."

"Why should you care? What you did to Hiroki Kogi wasn't polite."

Akira glared at me. "He deserved a few punches. Giving my name to the cops! When my mother heard we were behind it all, she hit me hard!"

"The problem isn't limited to what you did on Friday. You did something on Saturday morning, too."

"I didn't do anything on Saturday! I didn't even see Hiroki!"

"You saw him at school," I pointed out.

"No. Hiroki didn't come to school. There was an empty desk between Yukio and me. Ask Miss Ito. She records attendance during our homeroom meeting."

"Okay," I said, thinking that fact would be easy enough to check. "But if Hiroki ran away and was hurt or killed, don't you think it's your responsibility?"

"I'm not a bully," Akira said sharply.

"How would you feel if you were in Hiroki's position—if just because you were small and had studied abroad, you were tormented?"

Akira reeled back. "You're—You're not going to tell the coach, are you? I swear to you—I swear I'll never touch Hiroki-san again. I'll just study and play sports and be a good boy. I promise!"

A tittering sound arose. I hadn't realized that a handful of students were behind me, listening to the conversation. I'd wanted to keep things private, but now I realized that the students' sympathies were against Akira. I decided to play the scene for all it was worth and added, "There's a possibility that you and Yukio will never have another chance with Hiroki. If he's dead, there's no chance."

Akira said in a low voice, "I never thought something like this could happen to me."

"Don't think about *you*. Think about Hiroki." I walked away without a glance back, part of my act-tough strategy. But Akira's and Yukio's stories matched. They had an alibi.

I used a pay phone outside the school to telephone Miss Ito. She was home, and when she heard about Hiroki's disappearance, she gasped.

"It's my fault. I should have listened to you last week. I'm sorry," Miss Ito said.

"Was Hiroki in class Saturday morning?" I asked, just to make sure Akira and Yukio had told the truth.

"No. I recorded his absence in my attendance book, and later I checked in the office, and I heard his mother hadn't called in. Very strange—an unexcused absence from such a good student."

"The thing that's strange to me is that he rode the bus to school," I said.

"Hmm. Perhaps he exited the bus before it reached school and went somewhere else?"

"Such as?" This was an interesting idea.

"Maybe . . . he wanted to go to the train station. Either because he was running away, or because he thought of suicide. There was a boy who jumped the tracks there last year and died."

"He never seemed suicidal to me."

"How do you know? He was undoubtedly unhappy, and he has probably read about the many cases of students throughout our country who committed suicide after being bullied."

"Impossible," I said, my stomach lurching at the horrible vision she'd created for me. "If he'd jumped, we'd all know about it. That's the kind of thing that makes the news."

"Perhaps he changed his mind at the last minute. He might have just run away."

"Yes, that's what I'm thinking. He could be in a place where he feels safe."

"This is just awful." Miss Ito's voice trembled. "We should call the headmaster."

"Do you want me to do it?" I asked.

"Oh, no. I'll take care of the problem. Miss Shimura, I'm sorry. I didn't show compassion before. I want to make right what is wrong."

"Something terrible has happened," Mrs. Kogi wailed when I telephoned her. "We have found a letter in our mailbox from some people who say they are Hiroki's kidnappers! They really must have him because Hiroki's wristwatch was included."

"Quiet!" Mr. Kogi's voice came across in the background. "We cannot tell anyone about the note or Hiroki will be killed!"

Again I wondered at Hiroki's father's manner. Had he engineered his son's disappearance? It would have been so easy for him to slip a letter into his own mailbox. I wanted to see the letter.

"May I please come?" I asked again.

At last Mr. Kogi agreed, and half an hour later I was in their house. Mrs. Kogi had placed the letter in the center of the dining table. It was a single page of lightweight white paper covered by a mimeographed message typed in tiny *kanji*. It reminded me of the papers I had to deal with at Makigahara High School—the missives written in a code I couldn't break because of my language impairment.

I handed it back. "I'm sorry. Even though I speak Japanese, I cannot read much."

"But you're a teacher! You assign essays to the students!" Mr. Kogi's eyebrows rose.

"I ask them to write in a phonetic script so that I can understand."

"I will read aloud to Miss Shimura then," Mrs. Kogi looked at her husband defiantly. "It says:

> *'To the Kogi family. We have Hiroki, and will elimi-*
> *nate him if necessary to achieve our goal. If you wish*
> *to see your son again, you must deliver twenty-seven*
> *million yen by four A.M. Monday morning. Leave the*
> *sum in ten-thousand-yen notes in an envelope de-*
> *posited in the can return section of the Asahi Beer*
> *vending machine near the bus stop. No police, or*
> *your son dies.'* "

"It could be a terrorist cult," Mr. Kogi said. "They might have chosen me because they think I can take the money from the bank. But actually, I'd have to apply for a loan, like everyone else."

"We must do that," Mrs. Kogi said. "But who could give us money today? It's impossible!"

Twenty-seven million yen, a little less than $270,000, was an odd amount to request. Something about the letter nagged at me. I laid it down and turned to Mr. Kogi.

"Do you have to wait until Monday to access your loan files?"

"Not really. Because of my position, I do some work from home. I have the ability to get to my files, but not anyone else's."

"Could you pull up the names of everyone who applied for mortgage amounts of twenty-seven million in the last year?"

"You mean the people whom I approved?" Mr. Kogi asked.

"No. The ones you rejected."

It took Mr. Kogi an hour to come up with a list. We scrolled down the list of names until I saw one that I recognized, next to a mortgage of 27 million yen turned down because of a poor credit rating.

The police allowed the Kogis and me to ride in their van to Miss Ito's apartment building in a dreary section of Yokohama. Miss Ito only answered the door after the police threatened to bang it down. I looked past her into the tiny, crowded room. The walls were discolored from old leaks, and there was an unpleasant smell. An old woman who was stretched out on a sofa that took up most of the room's space entreated us to enter and drink tea. Miss Ito's mother clearly had no idea what was going on. I was struck by the poignancy of her situation, especially in light of what would happen to her daughter.

"Where is Hiroki Kogi?" the detective asked Miss Ito, who was standing like a sentry in the doorway.

"I left him at the school," she said coldly. "I would have kept him with me if my place was bigger. But as you see, it's quite miserable."

"Left him? You mean my son is dead!" Mr. Kogi shouted, emotion finally breaking through his salaryman's veneer of calm.

"No, I'm sure your precious son is healthy!" Miss Ito snapped back at him. "You are overreacting to the whole situation."

"How could you think that you'd get away with this kind of thing and keep teaching at the high school?" I asked. "Surely Hiroki would have told."

Miss Ito smiled tightly. "No, he wouldn't. I promised him that in exchange for spending some quiet time at school, I'd ensure that Yukio and Akira would be expelled."

I remembered that Hiroki hadn't told his parents the bullies' names. Many adolescents were afraid to talk to their parents about their problems. Miss Ito, with her years of experience teaching, understood.

"Why are you here, Shimura-san?" Miss Ito asked angrily while she was being handcuffed. "I told you not to bother about Hiroki."

"I guessed that the ransom note came from a teacher when I saw it was mimeographed just like the other school papers," I said. "But it wasn't until I learned that Mr. Kogi had turned you down for a mortgage that I knew for sure."

The officers searched Miss Ito's apartment anyway. It took all of two minutes, and sure enough, Hiroki wasn't there. Duties were delegated—two officers would take Miss Ito to the police station, while the Kogis and I would ride with two officers to the school, with an ambulance meeting us there.

Let him still be alive, I prayed to myself. I'd read an article in the newspaper about a schoolboy rolled up in a gym mat by bullies and stuck in a closet, where he died.

Our arrival with sirens blaring drew all the attention away from the high school's baseball game. A crowd tried to follow us inside the school, but a policeman barred the way. I ran alongside two of the officers, showing them the way to the music room. In the back was a closet, as Miss Ito had described.

"Don't be afraid! We are police here to help you," an officer called as he began rattling the knob of the locked closet door. There was no answer, and I felt my spirits sink. Hiroki probably was dead.

The officers were using so much force on the door that the lock plate came off. At last the door opened. Inside the small, dark space, there were stacked-up cardboard boxes, but no boy.

Had Miss Ito lied? No, I thought, seeing some plaster on the floor. I looked up and saw that a tile in the ceiling was slightly askew. I said, "He's gone through the ceiling!"

The police removed the tile, but nobody was narrow enough to fit through the narrow duct.

"He hasn't called out to us. That must mean he's lying dead inside the space!" Mrs. Kogi said. For the first time, Mr. Kogi put his arm around her.

"What if he found some way up to the roof?" I asked.

"No, no. Impossible," said the policeman, though he did make a move to call a janitor.

"Come on, let's see if there are any outlets on the roof," I encouraged the Kogis, but only Mrs. Kogi was willing to follow.

The two of us ran downstairs and out into the school-yard, where we stepped into a scene of pandemonium. The hundreds of teenagers who had been watching the baseball game were now crowded onto a section of blacktop near the school's west side. As I walked toward them I over-heard their frantic cries.

"Be careful!"

"We called the fire department on our cell phones! They're coming to rescue you!"

I looked up and saw a boy standing with his feet firmly planted on the roof.

"Here I am!" Hiroki called out, waving to me and his mother. He sounded strong, and happy.

As the students on the ground waved back and cheered Hiroki, I realized that this was the first chance the short boy had ever literally been in the position to look down on others. I had a feeling that once the news hit the paper, his celebrity stature would continue to grow.

I couldn't wait for class on Monday morning.

Katherine Hall Page writes a young-adult series called Christie & Company, and won the Agatha for her first book featuring caterer and minister's wife Faith Fairchild, The Body in the Belfry. *Since then Faith has appeared in ten books, including* The Body in the Big Apple. *The main character in this story by Page decides to become a widower—with unexpected results . . .*

The Would-Be Widower

Katherine Hall Page

Mr. Carter wanted to be a widower. And, since he already had a wife, he figured he was halfway there.

The idea of bereavement was irresistible. At meals, sitting across the table from his wife, he would indulge in rosy reverie, picturing especially those first days—the steady stream of comfort flowing into his house in the form of sympathetic friends bearing casseroles and baked goods. He would be stoic, breaking down only occasionally to shed some tears and whisper, "Why? Why?"

His new status would confer instant membership into

151

the club that he knew from careful observation yielded invitations to dinner, parties, plays, concerts, cruises, and bed from widows, divorcées, the never marrieds. An unattached man of his age in decent health, still with all his own teeth, was a rarity. He was his own best capital, and he longed to spend it. Mourning beckoned with all the promise of a new day. Besides, he loathed his wife.

Mabel had been a secretary at the small family-owned insurance agency where Mr. Carter, not part of the family, had worked all his adult life. Two years ago he'd been forced to retire by the grandson of the founder, a kid he used to entertain by pulling nickels from his ears. Apparently, Mr. Carter's inability to master the new technology, go with the flow on the information highway, made him a liability instead of an asset. The fact that most of his accounts had gone to the great big actuarial table in the sky had also hastened his departure.

Mabel hadn't been a family member either. She'd come in off the street to apply for the position after Mr. Carter had been working there ten years or so. She was a cute little thing then. "Petite," not "short"—she was quick to correct anyone who made the mistake. She was quick to correct any mistakes, Mr. Carter discovered shortly, not petitely, after their marriage. She was quick to learn new things too. She'd had no trouble moving first from a manual to electric typewriter, then finally to a word processor. She tossed words like "gigabyte" and "RAM" around with aplomb. "It's so simple, Charles. Children four and five years old, younger even, use computers all the time. I should think a man in his sixties would have no trouble."

He'd given it a shot, and after a while hit a key plunging the screen into darkness or producing ominous messages with fused bomb icons. It was after one of these episodes, which took one of the younger agents in the office an hour to rectify, that retirement was strongly suggested. Forty years. No gold watch. No testimonial dinner. Squat. Mabel, who'd decided to retire at the same time over the protests of her boss, got a dozen long-stemmed American Beauty roses and a cut-glass Waterford vase. "Very tasteful," she'd pronounced.

Yes, she'd been a cute little thing, but as the years went by, only "little" remained. She had always been plagued with allergies, and as a consequence, her nose was red, her face pinched and eyes watery. She kept tissues stuffed up her sleeves. It drove Mr. Carter crazy to see them sticking out from her cuffs, bits of white—wet with mucus. After Mabel stopped working, she stopped dressing up and replaced the suits and high heels she'd favored with sweats and athletic shoes. "Why not be comfortable?" she said, and ridiculed the way he kept his closetful of suits brushed, his wing tips polished. He wore the khakis and plaid sport shirts previously reserved for weekends every day now, but each Sunday he put on one of his suits for church, rotating it to the end of the row when he took it off. Mabel had stopped going to church. "I can talk to God anywhere." She used the time for her daily power walk. She was constantly urging him to join her and do something other than sit indoors and read. "If not walking, then go to a gym. Anything but vegetate. You don't even have a hobby!" Mabel's hobby was her garden. She grew flowers and more produce than they could ever eat, crowding the chest freezer in the basement, next to the pails of mushrooms she tended, with lima beans, stewed tomatoes, and other things Mr. Carter disliked eating.

Mr. Carter didn't feel the need of a gym. He weighed the same as he had the day he was married. And he did get out of the house. He walked to the library. And sometimes he took the bus and went to one of the museums in Boston. His hobbies were reading, he told Mabel, and art. She would snort at his answer. "You're supposed to produce something with a hobby. Besides, reading doesn't count. Anybody can read."

Maybe he wouldn't hate her so much if they'd had children, but Mabel hadn't been too keen on the idea, and then when she'd grudgingly given in, they couldn't. "It wasn't meant to be," she told anyone bold enough to inquire. He supposed he could have divorced her, but he'd been busy at work and their nightly interactions had been brief, limited to a quick dinner before he settled in with his book and she with her seed catalogues. And what would have been the grounds? Drippy nose? Bossiness? Lima beans? More important, "divorced" was not as desirable as "widowed." Divorced meant something had been wrong with your marriage, that maybe *you* had done something wrong. It wasn't the image he wanted for himself. And it wasn't true.

Maybe he wouldn't hate her so much if she'd kept working. It was her constant presence that was driving him mad. He'd suggested she think about taking a part-time job, not let her skills go to waste. He'd liked the phase and repeated it. "Why on earth would I want to go back to work?" she said. "I've worked all my life. Now it's my time." She sounded like a television commercial, "Now It's My Time." It was after the third repetition of the phrase that he decided to kill her.

It felt good to have a goal. He was happier than he'd been in many years. He was glad now that they hadn't had a family. He wouldn't have been able to deprive children of a mother, or grandchildren of a grandmother. And their own families posed no problems. Both his and her parents had died years ago. Mr. Carter was an only child, and Mabel had an older sister living in Canada. The two had never been close and Mabel didn't even know whether the woman was still alive. So there would be no relatives to question the sudden death of a beloved family member.

It would have to be a perfect crime. That went without

saying. He would immediately be the prime suspect. It's always the husband. He'd read enough mysteries and true crime books to know that. Well, maybe not always, but usually. There was no point in going through with it if he wasn't going to be able to reap the benefits of being a widower. Much as he disliked living with Mabel, it was preferable to prison. He knew there was a risk, but oh the rewards!

After the food and the calls tapered off, he saw himself joining one of those grief support groups, basking in the pathos of others like himself. He would go on Elderhostels to Tuscany and Prague—places he had only read about. Places Mabel had never cared to visit. "If you want greasy Italian food, you can get all you want in the North End. Besides, you have to bring your own water and toilet paper. Who needs that?" He would date attractive women with beautifully coiffed silver hair. Women who wore scent and took the trouble to apply flawless makeup. He would get subscription tickets for the symphony. His own seats. He would nod to those around him, careful not to be too familiar. He would maintain his aura, his dignity. They would nod back, commenting to each other in low voices about the well-dressed elderly gentleman, retired businessman no doubt—or perhaps an academic. After the concert he and his lady friend—he liked the sound of that—would have supper at the Café Budapest, romantic places, and when he took her home, she would invite him in for coffee. She'd offer decaf, but he'd smile and say he could handle the real thing. She'd laugh and he would kiss her. He could close his eyes even now and feel the warmth and softness of her skin on his lips. They would go to bed and she would protest that her body was not what it had been when she was young. He would whisper that if anything she must be more beautiful. They would make love. And sleep long and dreamlessly, waking in each other's arms. She would not blow her nose. She would not say they were too old for such nonsense. She would not laugh at Mr. Carter's naked body nor comment that his skin seemed to have grown too large for his bones. She would not move into the guest room and call it hers.

Mr. Carter didn't own a gun or a weapon of any kind, although Mabel kept her clippers and some of her other garden tools razor sharp. But he couldn't shoot her—the police would see through the "I thought she was a burglar" story in a flash—nor could he fake her suicide. There was the whole problem of powder burns. They'd have to be on her hand, not his, and he didn't think he could get Mabel to hold a gun and pull the trigger. Possibly he could drug her, then, using gloves, put the weapon in her hand and maneuver her finger to fire the shot. This might just do the trick, but the gun would of course be traced back to him. He'd have to buy one at a gun shop or from a pawnbroker since he didn't have any street connections. He supposed he could go into Boston at night and try to purchase one, but he might also get himself mugged or even killed, which would spoil everything. And as for the garden tools, it was highly unlikely that Mabel could be induced to decapitate herself. She could, however, have an accident with her chipper, getting her hand stuck as she fed in leaves and branches, then bleed to death. He filed the notion away for further thought.

After reviewing his options over some weeks, Mr. Carter came to the conclusion that the simpler the method, the better. No weapons, poisons, lethal machinery. He'd take Mabel to the mountains and push her off a cliff. Hikers had accidents all the time. Especially novices, which they were. He'd have no trouble convincing her to go. She wanted him to exercise and she wanted him to have a hobby. Hiking would be his new love, and he wasted no time in preparing the groundwork.

"Mabel," he told her at dinner, one of her more inspired efforts—scrod baked in canned cream of mushroom soup, the current crop of her own mushrooms still in a state of immaturity. "You're right. I do need to get out more, but walking would bore me. I'd rather look at the beauty of nature than rows of houses and passing cars. I'm going to take up hiking."

He had expected an enthusiastic response, but this was Mabel.

"It's not as easy as you think. You'll need to get proper hiking boots, for a start."

"Already in my closet. I went to Eastern Mountain Sports this afternoon. And I took out a membership in the Appalachian Mountain Club. I should be getting maps and guides soon. Meanwhile I'll start with some of the little hills around here. If you'd care to join me, I'd be delighted."

"I'll get some boots."

He took a large bite of the fish. Whatever firmness of flesh it had possessed in the wild had been destroyed in Mabel's preparation and it was almost as liquid as the sauce. He smacked his lips. His heart was full and he gazed at his wife gratefully. "Wonderful," he said. "Absolutely wonderful."

It had been a mild winter, hardly any snow. Global warming, Mr. Carter supposed, but it provided excellent hiking weather, and in the following weeks he and his spouse attempted ever hardier climbs with frequent day trips to the mountains in New Hampshire. He was surprised to find himself enjoying the exercise, noting the first signs of spring and gradually adopting Mabel's hunter-gatherer habits. She was a firm disciple of Euell Gibbons, masticating sassafras leaves, pouncing on acorns to grind for bread and muffins, and scooping wintergreen leaves for tea into one of the Ziploc bags she always carried in her rucksack. Knowing she would soon be gone granted him tolerance and the odd moment of affection for his wife. It would all be put to good use when he played the part of the lonely, grieving widower.

When spring began to give way to summer, they tackled the White Mountains. Mr. Carter had studied the AMC guides and maps until he knew every trail, every outcropping, every precipice with the precision of blind fingers over Braille. At last he decided they were ready—his goal: the top of the head wall on the Tuckerman Ravine Trail on Mount Washington. Since he'd read in the guide that Mount Washington had claimed more lives than any other peak in North America, the trail had beckoned like Shangri-la, its image a haunting melody during every hike, a coda to his footfalls. He booked a room, twin beds, at an inn in nearby Jackson for five days. It would be their anniversary gift to each other, he told Mabel. A sentimental gesture.

Their anniversary fell on Thursday, and if luck was with him, so would Mabel. It wouldn't do to arrive and kill her immediately. He would need to establish themselves as an affable—and devoted—couple. Two people enjoying retirement and each other. Two people with a new hobby. Two people who might get into trouble in the mountains.

When the day came, it was perfect. At breakfast some of the other guests remarked on the weather and hastened away to prepare for their own outings. It would seem that the paths would be crowded, not a moment of privacy, but Mr. Carter wasn't worried. He'd checked the conditions carefully. The ski season, which continued well into the spring at this elevation, had ended. School was still in session, so no intrepid von Trapp–type families would get in the way, and he'd avoided the weekend, which would bring more people to the popular trail. A moment was all he needed, and he was sure he would get it.

"Shall we, my dear?" he asked playfully as his wife finished her stewed prunes.

Soon they were on the trail, a more difficult one than they had attempted before. A challenge. He was positively giddy with joy. The sky was blue. Not a single cloud. The hours passed swiftly, and then, unless he was wrong, five more minutes would bring them to the spot he'd selected. A fabulous view. He owed her that at least. They were above the timberline. No trees to grab on the way down. That was for him.

And it all went according to plan.

"Why don't we stop a moment? The footing's a little tricky here and I want to rest," he told her. "Besides, it's spectacular." He swept his arm out encompassing the surrounding peaks—the Wildcat Range opposite—and the valley, far, far below. Then swept his arm back, neatly knocking her off her small feet and sending her hurtling over the edge, crying "Watch out!" at the same time for her sake—and the sake of others on the trail out of sight, but not earshot.

It was done. He was free. He was falling.

She had grabbed him by the ankle. She was taking him with her. His fury knew no bounds. Then, nothing.

The next thing he knew he was strapped to a stretcher and a ranger was telling him to lie still, he'd be all right. "Looks like you broke a leg, but you're a very lucky man."

"My wife, what about my wife?" Mr. Carter asked.

"She's fine, a bit bruised and shaken up, of course. You landed on a small projection thirty feet down. It's a miracle. We lost a hiker from that very spot a year ago. Your wife's just ahead of us. Didn't hit her head the way you did, still they'll want to check her out at the hospital." The other ranger broke in, admonishing him, "I hope you understand you folks could have been killed. Your wife mentioned you've just started climbing. It's treacherous up here, especially with all the loose rock after the snow's melted." She repeated the other ranger's words, "You're a very lucky man."

Mr. Carter groaned and let himself slip back into unconsciousness.

He hadn't broken a leg. Just his ankle. It gave him plenty of time to think. Maybe simple hadn't been such a good idea. He'd have to come up with something a bit more complicated than a shove—something a bit more sure. His wife was busy in the garden from morning to night, so there was that to be thankful for. While she was out at the nursery getting more manure, he hobbled to the shed in the backyard and looked at the assortment of things she used to keep weeds and garden pests away. Virtually every preparation carried the skull and crossbones logo he'd been conjuring up as he sat indoors reading. Then there was the chipper. It was in the corner with her small rototiller. The good old chipper. He gazed longingly at the poisons again. "Last meal for slugs," read one. Last meal for Mabel. But unless he could convince the police she was suicidal, the use of any of these goodies would immediately be traced back to him. He felt like a kid in a candy store with empty pockets. He turned and went back to the house. His ankle was throbbing.

The whole thing would be much easier if he were less of a gentleman, he thought bitterly. He wanted to kill his wife, but he didn't want her to know he had. Let her go to her grave firm in the belief that she'd had a good marriage. It would be unspeakably boorish to behave otherwise. If he hadn't cared about protecting her, he could simply have smothered her with a pillow and arranged the whole thing to look like an allergy attack. She'd certainly had some severe ones, and was allergic to everything from dust to bee stings.

Day after day he turned the problem over and over in his

mind. He couldn't arrange a car accident. Mabel had never learned to drive, and besides, he hadn't the faintest notion how to cut brake cables or whatever it was they were always doing in books. It got to the point where he couldn't sleep at night. His ankle bothered him. It had been a nasty break and the pain matched the pain in his aching brain. After the fourth night in a row with scant rest, he called the doctor, and that afternoon the drugstore delivered some chloral hydrate. He opened the bottle and sniffed. It smelled like cherry syrup. Not unpleasant at all. Then he read the lengthy printout—from a computer, of course—that listed the recommended dosage and all the side effects. He supposed the drug companies covered themselves this way. Terrify the consumer with a smorgasbord of alarming symptoms so no one could sue. He read through the "Do not combine with alcohol" and "Do not operate heavy machinery" warnings, getting to the "May cause skin rash, mental confusion, ataxia"—he'd have to look that up—"headache, nausea, dizziness, drowsiness"—well, wasn't that the whole point?—"stupor, depression, irritability, poor judgment, neglect of personal appearance"—they were really covering themselves here, and then a catchall—"central nervous system depression." He went to the bookshelves and took down Webster's. "Ataxia"—loss of the ability to control muscle movement.

He put the book back in its place and went back to his armchair, wending his way through the jungle of Mabel's plants that filled the room. He picked up the bottle and held it to the light, watching the way the sun made a bright red blotch on the morning paper. Chloral hydrate. Just what the doctor ordered.

Mr. Carter hadn't mentioned his sleeplessness to his wife, nor his subsequent call to the doctor. Now he congratulated himself on his discretion. It was almost as if his unconscious mind was taking over and charting the right course. His conscious mind had simply not wanted to talk to Mabel. She wasn't a drinker, but she liked to indulge herself every now and then with a liqueur after dinner. He found the peppermint schnapps, melon liqueurs, and cherry brandies she favored nauseatingly sweet. If he kept her company, which he seldom did, he sipped a small snifter of cognac. Mabel made herself concoctions poured over crushed ice, drinking from their everyday tumblers. "It's the same drink in a jelly glass or your precious crystal," she pointed out. They hadn't received many wedding gifts when they'd married, and the crystal had been from his parents. Mabel had managed to break most of it over the years, and he washed it himself now. Maybe if it had been from her parents, she'd have felt differently. They'd given the newlyweds a check—a rather small one.

He bided his time. Each night he measured out his dose—and didn't take it. When he had accumulated what would surely be enough, he put his plan into action.

"You've worked hard all day, my dear," he said after dinner—Mabel's famous "Vegetable Stew," a mélange of whatever was ripe dumped into the pressure cooker— "why don't I make you a drink? I'm going to have one myself."

Mabel thought that would be nice. She was still in her gardening clothes, although her hands were clean, scrubbed raw, the nails chipped. Gloves were a bother and got in her way.

He went to the kitchen, thinking paradoxically that a truly thoughtful wife would offer to fetch the libations herself rather than be waited upon by her handicapped husband. She had been typically unsympathetic about the injury and had expressed her opinion several times too often that he needed to walk more or his muscles would be even weaker. He reached for the glass she liked and, using the ice maker on the refrigerator door, filled it. He took the chloral hydrate from behind the flour canister where he'd placed it earlier in the day and poured it, filling half the tumbler. The dose the doctor had prescribed was two teaspoons before bedtime. Mr. Carter was both taller and heavier than his wife; most people were. With the addition of the cherry brandy, the drink should send her swiftly to sleep, and then with any luck into a deadly coma. He planned to put her to bed, inhaler on the floor by her side, apparently knocked out of reach. Unlike the pillow method, she'd never know what hit her. The perfect crime. He'd be certain to mention the brandy to whomever responded to the 911 call he'd make in the morning after failing to rouse her and noting with horror the absence of all vital signs. No one would suspect the chloral hydrate, but if it was found, he'd been taking his medicine as ordered each night, and there was his name on the half-empty bottle to prove it. But he doubted it would come to that. If Mabel and he had been younger, perhaps there would be some suspicions, but at their age people did die, especially people with severe allergy-induced asthma.

He topped off the drink with the sweet brandy and poured himself a more generous than usual amount of Rémy Martin. He had heard that it was what the cognac connoisseurs drank. It was expensive enough, certainly. Carrying the two glasses, he made his way back into the living room, emphasizing the awkwardness of his cast as he approached Mabel's chair.

She was reading *The Encyclopedia of Plant Lore,* a gift from him several Christmases ago. She snapped it shut and took her drink. "Yum." She smiled appreciatively, and by the time he reached his own chair and turned around to face her, she'd quaffed more than half of it. He started to chide her. Really, it was most unbecoming to watch a woman swill alcohol that way, but stopped himself. The quicker the better. The quicker the deader.

"Cheers," he said, and lifted his glass. She set hers down and picked up the book again. Was it his imagination or did she seem unusually flushed? He held his breath and put his cognac down. Tonight of all nights he needed a clear head. Tonight! His blood raced. It would be tonight.

Probably the first person he'd call after the emergency number would be Mrs. Parsons, who lived next door. They had been neighbors for thirty years, and when Mr. Parsons had been alive, the two couples occasionally played bridge. They were pleasant enough, but fully occupied in bringing up their four children. Mrs. Parsons had put on considerable weight since the death of her husband, and an endless stream of children and grandchildren were in and out of the house. She was a good cook, judging from the Christmas cookies and Fourth of July blueberry pie she bestowed upon them each year. He could count on her for any number of meals and other forms of sustenance.

He let his mind drift to the next few days. Tomorrow would be the worst—or the best, depending upon one's viewpoint. There would be the police rescue squad, then when it became apparent that it was alas too late, he'd have to deal with the Medical Examiner, or perhaps it would be their own doctor. He'd be finding out soon. Then arrangements with the funeral home, and he had no doubt that the Reverend Dobbins would arrive with words of comfort immediately. Mr. Carter thought "For the Beauty of the Earth" would be an appropriate hymn for Mabel's service. He'd leave the rest to Reverend Dobbins. Interment was no problem. They had a plot, purchased years ago. He'd have his own name carved on the headstone too, with his birth date and the rest blank. Although, if he remarried, that might hurt his next wife's feelings. Just Mabel's, then, with an appropriate epitaph. Best not to burn one's bridges. Word would get around. The phone, which seldom rang, would ring off the hook. He'd ask one of the women in the church to help him plan a suitable collation for after the service. Lilies, not gladiolas . . .

"I think I'll go to bed. Kinda tired." Mabel's speech was definitely slurred. She stood up and knocked into the Benjamin fig tree next to her chair as she stepped toward the stairs.

"Are you all right, my dear?"

"Fine. Need to sleep, that's all."

He lingered for a moment, enjoying the emptiness of the room and the prospect of the continued void in his future, then went to bed himself. He set the alarm for three o'clock—enough time for the lethal cocktail to have worked, and time to set the stage.

When it sounded, he walked soundlessly down the carpeted hall and opened the door to his wife's room. For a moment he felt a twinge of regret as he gazed at the still figure in the bed, but it passed immediately and he found he had a sudden desire to laugh with glee. But that would be unseemly. He composed his face into a proper widower's expression and approached Mabel's corpse. The inhaler was on her bedside table within arm's reach. He reached to move it and fling the bedclothes about a bit, then froze.

"What do you think you're doing?" Mabel sat up in bed, her face an angry mask. "I thought I made it clear, we're past that sort of thing."

Fright turned to stunned surprise and he gulped for words, unable to utter the ones racing through his head. How could she possibly have drunk the mixture and be alive? And awake!

"Thought I heard you call, my dear," he mumbled. "Must have been dreaming." He hastened out of the room, pulling the door firmly shut. Yes, he had been dreaming, and awakened to a nightmare.

Mr. Carter was a persistent man. He had been successful

at his job not because of hard or soft sell, but persistent sell. He possessed the ability to wait. Rebuffed by potential clients, he'd call two years later, and like as not sign new customers, dissatisfied with the coverage they'd purchased instead. Most of the population regarded insurance companies as potential adversaries and it wasn't difficult to get them to switch loyalties with a few well-chosen aspersions. Therefore, when he awoke the next morning, he was calm. True, he had expected to be widowed by the end of the summer, but these things took time. He'd taken to reading the obituaries and news reports of fatal accidents for ideas. Most involved automobiles, but one day he happened upon a column describing, with some humor, what a death trap one's home was.

He read eagerly, eliminating household poisons, ladders, and carbon monoxide as unsuitable for his purpose. The section his eyes lingered lovingly over involved electrical appliances and water. He should have thought of it before. It wasn't as kind as the other approaches, but Mabel was making things difficult. However, there was always the chance that it would be so quick, she wouldn't realize what was happening. Several years ago they had indulged themselves with a whirlpool tub, or rather, Mabel had. Mr. Carter never used it, finding the jets of water disconcerting and the noise it made annoying. All he had to do was plug in a radio and drop it into the tub. She wouldn't hear him come into the bathroom, and by the time she noticed, it would be too late. When the rescue squad came, he'd lament his wife's foolhardy habit of listening to music while she bathed and regret that he hadn't thought to give her one safe for such use. According to the newspaper, countless Americans died just this way each year. He folded the newspaper, put it in the recycle bin, and went out to the kitchen, where Mabel was putting lunch on the table. The garden was at its height and they seemed to have become vegetarians. He promised himself a thick steak after a suitable period of absence of appetite was observed.

A cold cream soup and salad awaited. Recently some of Mabel's efforts had not gone down so well, and he was relieved to see plain fare. She was slicing some zucchini bread, warm from the oven.

"Looks delicious. Fruits of your labor. You've been hard at it, I can see. You should treat yourself to a long soak in the whirlpool, my dear."

Mabel said she thought that was a good idea and sat down.

Mr. Carter was spooning the last drops of the soup, leek, he thought, when he felt himself breaking out in a cold sweat. He looked up at his wife in alarm. His heart suddenly seemed to have stopped beating and he was terribly dizzy. He tried to get up and a wave of nausea passed over him. The vomit rose in his throat, but he managed to gasp, "What was it?"

"Oleander. Mimics a heart attack. Sorry it had to be this way, but nothing else was working."

His gaze was clouding over, yet he still managed a smile. A big smile. A wasp had landed unnoticed on Mabel's arm, bare in her sleeveless shirt. Another joined it, drawn by the smell of the bread on the table. He closed his eyes, faintly hearing her startled cries.

Early on he'd replaced the epinephrine in her syringes with saline.

Luck had been with him after all.

*Anne Perry lives in Scotland and is well-known for her two Victorian series, one with Superintendent Thomas Pitt and his clever wife Charlotte; the other with private investigator William Monk and his bride, nurse Hester Latterly. Perry was nominated twice for the Agatha Award for Best Novel for two Monk books—*The Face of a Stranger *and* Defend and Betray*—and won the Edgar Award for Best Short Story for "Heroes." This charming story is inspired by Perry's own menagerie and features Daisy, the sensible, if four-footed, detective.*

Daisy and the Christmas Goose

Anne Perry

I was lying in my basket beside the stove in the kitchen one evening a little before last Christmas, having nice dreams about puddings and such like things, when my half sister, Willow, came and sat down on top of me. It woke me up with a start, because of the disgusting smell! Not a decent dog smell, like pond mud or manure, or dead mice;

168

rather more like the cupboard under the sink, sort of sharp and stinging the nose.

Bertie, who is my friend and ally, but rather too self-important for a cat, came sauntering across the kitchen table, wrinkling his nose.

"That is disgusting!" he said with feeling. "Did Boss take you to see Kenny again?"

Then I realized what sort of smell it was. Kenny is our vet. He is very nice, but I don't like the smell of his rooms, and sometimes he pokes needles into us.

"No she didn't!" Willow said indignantly. "I've been here all day! I was helping Roddy prune Friend's roses."

Actually she was waiting for him to throw sticks for her, but no one bothered to point that out, except Lottie, and we ignore her. Lottie is one of Boss's rescues. She was found in a coal yard about two weeks ago, and since Boss will give anything a home, we are obliged to put up with her. She was filthy and sick and covered with fleas when she came, and of course very tiny. Now she's a bit cleaner and fatter, but still has a terrible temper. She's about eight weeks old, we think.

"That doesn't make sense," I pointed out to Willow. "You smell like the vet's room."

"That's the geese," Willow replied.

Casper got off the pine chest where he sits to look out of the window, and came over, curiosity all over his spotty face. He says he's mostly a pointer, but he looks like a dalmation to me, except his legs are too long. But his legs are too long for any kind of a dog.

"What are geese?" he asked, looking at me as if I should know. Actually I am the senior dog here and it's my job to keep everyone in order, which is a very great responsibility, when Boss will bring creatures like Lottie home, without asking me. I don't know exactly what a goose is, but it would have been very demeaning to admit that in front of everyone.

"What have geese got to do with it?" I said instead.

"Roddy has some," Willow replied.

"How do you know?"

"Because he was telling those two boys about them," she said.

The boys she was referring to came up from the village to help Boss tidy up the garden for the winter, rake up leaves and make sure the fences are strong, and that kind of thing.

"Then you should know what they are," Bertie said, washing his tail.

"You should know!" Lottie added, taking a swipe at him with her paw and, luckily for her, missing.

"He likes them a lot," Willow said, as if that were an answer.

"Roddy likes all sorts of things," I pointed out. "He likes you, and that friend of his who was up in the garden talking to him today."

"He paid for Herbie's sore foot," she told us.

"Who is Herbie?"

"One of his geese, of course!"

Then I remembered. I sat up and looked at Casper. "Geese fly," I told him. "In the spring and the autumn. In skeins across the sky. They honk, and their wings creak. You can hear them."

"Oh." He looked totally confused. So was I, but I decided to go to sleep again before anyone could ask me any more.

"Herbie's ointment fell out of his pocket." Willow curled herself up with her nose in her tail. "I picked it up. That's what it smells like."

"Herbie's foot must be very sore," Bertie said, "to need something that smells like that!"

* * *

It was not a very good night. Casper kept barking, but he barks at the wind, or the leaves, or even at nothing at all. I joined him once or twice. I really thought I heard something outside, but since Boss didn't come down, there was nothing to do about it anyway.

Then in the morning when Boss was downstairs to let us out, feed the chickens, the cats, and the little birds in the aviary, we knew what it was. We piled out at the back door and Casper went careering around the garden as usual on the frosty grass. Willow was still half asleep. But I knew there was something wrong . . . terribly wrong!

The Woofer Wagon was gone! Boss has a car for going out in, and for taking us to Kenny. But the Woofer Wagon is ours! I mean it belongs to the three of us, and to Tara next door, who lives with Friend, just across the driveway. It is for going to the beach in, and coming home again, of course, after we have had a swim. Nobody shouts about sand, or water, or feet or things, or even a scuffed or slightly chewed seat.

It was gone! There was an empty space on the drive where it should have been!

I started to bark, really loudly.

Boss called out to me to be quiet.

Willow, who had been standing there half asleep, woke up properly and realized what had happened. She began to howl. Casper joined in.

That brought Boss outside. She was just about to get really angry with us when she too realized that the Woofer Wagon was missing.

The first thing she did, even before giving us breakfast, was to telephone Friend and ask her to come over.

"It's been stolen!" she said as soon as Friend arrived, with Tara, who was naturally very upset too. She is a

Labrador, and loves to swim. She stood with her ears down and tail between her legs. I think she hadn't had any breakfast either.

"Who on earth would steal the Woofer Wagon?" Friend said in bewilderment. "I mean with the Jaguar only a few yards away from it!"

"It's stupid!" Boss said angrily. "I heard Casper barking, but I didn't take any notice! He barks at the wind."

"Well it wasn't the wind that took the Woofer Wagon," Friend said decisively. "I know it isn't worth a great deal, except to the dogs, but we should report it to the police anyway. How absolutely rotten! I hate to think anyone around here would do that!"

"It must be someone around here," Boss pointed out. "Who else would even know about it? There wouldn't be any passing strangers, because there's nowhere to pass to—except Rockfield, and that's only a dozen houses. What I don't understand is why take that old car when the Jaguar is right there too!"

We all trooped inside, Tara and Friend as well, and Boss called the police station in Tain and told them what had happened. Apparently, they said they would come and take a look at the situation. No one felt any better, except they did remember to give us breakfast.

Willow lay by the stove and wrapped herself up in her blanket. She was totally miserable. Casper sat on the pine chest and stared out of the window at the orchard, occasionally whimpering. Tara paced around until everyone shouted at her to sit down, which she did, sort of half. I tried to think of a plan, but nothing came into my head except how much we would miss the Woofer Wagon and our trips to the beach, and to see Mother Perry. Boss always told us not to swim in the pond up the field, but she lets us swim in the sea. I used to think I didn't like water, but now I love it! It's sort of wriggly and shimmery all over the skin, and nice and cool on the feet. And some of our best adventures began on the beach. This is altogether a very bad thing.

The police eventually came. Nobody else bothered to go out except Tara, who always goes with Friend, in case she might miss something, and me, because it is part of my job to know.

The police were surprised when boss told them what the Woofer Wagon was like, as if its being old and a trifle battered, and full of dogs' hair and paw marks, made it worse, not better!

Lottie came out and climbed up on the fence, parading along the top of it. She is turning into a show-off now that she is feeling well and thinks she belongs here! We have more than enough kittens! We didn't need another, especially one that spits at everybody as she does.

The policewoman admired her! I can't think why, except that she doesn't know her! She got scratched and bitten for her trouble, but she didn't seem to mind.

"Isn't she pretty now!" she said affectionately. "About eight or nine weeks?"

"Yes," Boss agreed. "She was found abandoned and starving in the coal yard, full of worms, poor little mite. But she's fine now."

The policeman looked puzzled. "I suppose they took it because you're far enough out of the village they wouldn't be seen, and from what you say, the car is pretty ordinary." He looked at Boss's car in the driveway; the Woofer Wagon is ours! "Not like the Jaguar," he went on. "People would remember that, I suppose. Well, Mrs. MacDonald, we'll make a note of it and let you know if we hear anything, but I expect it's just kids joyriding. It may turn up quite all right . . . somewhere. Glad you've got another one anyway. Bit stuck without a car all the way out here."

That was no comfort at all! We can't go to the beach in

the Jaguar! The only place we go to in that is to see Kenny if we're sick, or get needles! This was really a very miserable Christmas indeed!

In the afternoon, Roddy came up and we all sat in the kitchen being miserable.

"I don't know what it's coming to," he said, warming his hands around a mug of peppermint tea. "Who'd want to go and steal half a dozen geese!"

"Are all of them gone?" Friend asked. She had come over as well, and Tara.

"Yes. Even Herbie!" Roddy said dourly. "Some Christmas!"

"Well, if we're going to get them back, we'll have to think of something pretty soon," Boss said unhappily. "It's only four days till . . . till it's too late!"

"It'll be too late before that," Friend pointed out. "People are selling turkeys and geese from this weekend. That's when Sheena at the farm is doing hers."

Suddenly we understood this was even more terrible than the Woofer Wagon going missing. Willow opened her eyes and stared at Boss. Casper turned around from the window, where he was waiting for next door's dogs to show so he could bark at them. He looked horrified.

Tara turned to me. "They're going to eat Herbie?"

"Unless we do something," I answered.

Everyone sat up and took notice, even Lottie, who actually very seldom listened to anybody.

"What shall we do?" Willow asked anxiously.

I had no ideas yet. I wished I had not spoken so quickly.

"Who's going to look after his foot?" Casper asked. He thinks a lot about these things because he watches the vet programs on television, as long as the animals are there. He can't be bothered with people.

Willow opened her mouth to say that would hardly matter, in the circumstances, and I nipped her to be quiet. She squealed indignantly and I got told off, which was not fair. I settled down to think.

The next morning things got even worse, if that was possible. Boss came down to give everybody breakfast, and she couldn't find Lottie. Bertie heaved a sigh of relief. He doesn't have a lot of patience with kittens, and Lottie was just one too many, in all respects.

But Boss was terribly upset. She went all around the house calling for Lottie and moving things, opening cupboard doors and crawling on the floor to look under beds and all sorts of places Lottie's never even thought of going. She found one or two things she'd lost ages ago, but not Lottie.

Then she telephoned Friend, and she came over and they both hunted. I went with them to help, but it didn't do any good. Lottie had vanished.

We all went around the garden as well, hunting and calling and moving bits of wood and old boxes and other things waiting to be thrown out. It was horribly cold and a complete waste of time. Lottie was gone.

"There are thieves everywhere!" Willow said wretchedly. "First our Woofer Wagon, then Herbie and the other geese, and now Lottie!"

"What I don't understand," Bertie said, washing his paws, "is why anyone would take Lottie! Who'd want her?"

"Boss wanted her," Willow pointed out. "She took her from the coal yard."

"Boss rescued her!" Bertie corrected loftily. "Nobody needs rescuing from here!"

"Maybe they're rescuing us?" Casper suggested. He's had his nose scratched a number of times.

Boswell perked up at the idea. I don't know why, because he spends most of his time up the field hunting mice anyway, but I suppose in this weather he likes to be by the fire as much as we do.

Nobody answered him.

Boss and Friend were sitting gloomily at the kitchen table trying to think where else to search.

"She'll die in this cold," Boss said, staring out of the windows at the gray sky.

Friend didn't reply, which was unusual. She must have been very miserable indeed not to have said anything at all.

Roddy came up just before lunch. Nobody had found Herbie or any of his geese. The police telephoned to say they hadn't found the Woofer Wagon either, but wanted to know what it was worth.

It's worth a trip to the beach! And that's priceless.

"We've got to do something!" Willow insisted. "Everything is going wrong."

Because Friend was over with us, Tara was too, but she hadn't thought of anything, and neither had the cats. It was worth asking because Humphrey gets around quite a lot, looking for more breakfasts. Pansy was very old, like our Lewis, so she might have known something. She used to be a great hunter in her day: rats, pheasants, partridges, moles, rabbits, even a hare once, so she said. As well as all the usual mice and birds and so on. She and Lewis are the only ones who came up from the south, wherever that is. Thea, Friend's Siamese, came from Fort William, but I don't know where that is either.

"Maybe Fort William's like the coal yard?" Casper suggested.

Maybe it is. Thea has a temper like Lottie's, but on the other hand she has a pedigree longer than my tail, so she says, and the coal yard wouldn't do that.

"Why would anyone steal Lottie?" Tara said again. "Doesn't everybody have enough cats already?"

"They can't have known her!" Humphrey curled up on the table, having just eaten his third breakfast.

"That matters!" I realized. "Then it was a stranger. Why didn't we hear them, or smell them?"

"We didn't hear whoever took the Woofer Wagon," Willow pointed out.

"I did!" Casper put his nose between his paws. "I barked, and no one listened to me. You all told me to be quiet."

He was right. "I'm sorry," I apologized. It was the only fair thing to do.

He was very generous about it. "That's all right," he said airily. "You can't help it!"

Humphrey was still thinking about Lottie. "Did you hear anyone last night?" he asked Casper.

Casper looked very important. He thought hard for several moments while we all waited.

"No," he said at last. He looked disappointed, and lay down.

Suddenly I realized how important that was. "Then nobody came!" I said jubilantly. "She must be still here! We must all look again." I stood up, ready to begin.

"Lie down, Daisy!" Boss told me.

Naturally I ignored her and went to the door. The cats all went through the flap one after the other: Humphrey, Bertie, Boswell, Isadora, Cassandra, and Little Lily. I barked. Then Willow and Tara barked too, and Casper began to squeak and yip and jump up and down.

Boss said something very rude, but she let us out anyway. We went racing around the garden, around the sides and the front, the aviary which is all the cats' favorite place to visit and watch, in the hope that one day they'll find a way in, or one of the canaries will come out! It never happens.

We tried the chicken run as well, and were feeling disheartened by the time we ended up where all the rubbish was piled to go to the dump and be taken away. Of course, we didn't search the rest of the house inside because we weren't allowed upstairs, and neither would Lottie be.

We needed to get the boxes and boards down to search them properly.

"I like boxes," Isadora said, looking up at them.

"Everybody likes boxes," Bertie replied. "Boxes are very good for going to sleep in. The smaller the cozier."

"We should get them down," Boswell suggested. "Maybe Lottie is in a box?"

"We can't reach," I replied. "You climb up!"

"If they fall down, I shall fall with them," he said huffily.

Humphrey, who is so large, on account of living at both Friend's house and Boss's, and eating two of every meal, leaped up and sent the whole pile flying all over the place. Several of them nearly hit me; one caught Casper on the back, but it was empty, so I suppose it didn't matter.

One of the boxes rolled over and another box fell out of the inside. I went over to look at it, and felt sharp pins on my nose. I yelped and ran backward.

"Wonderful!" Willow said joyously.

I shook myself. "There's nothing wonderful about it!" I snapped.

"Yes there is! You've found Lottie!" Casper shouted, and he went racing round and round the garden as fast as he could go, yapping whenever he had the breath.

Lottie staggered out of the box, which was now almost upside down, and she stretched and blinked, and stretched again, a bit like a furry caterpillar, then stared at all of us.

"What?" she said huffily. "Why did you wake me up and tip me out? It's cold out here. And stop making that noise! Its hurts my head!"

Casper's yapping hurts everybody's head.

"We've found you!" Willow said delightedly, wagging her tail so hard it just about hit her around the ears.

"I wasn't lost!" Lottie snapped back in her usual manner. She started to wash her face.

"Yes, you were!" Willow refused to be discouraged . . . or contradicted.

"No I wasn't! I knew where I was."

"You don't count!" I told her sharply. "We didn't and Boss didn't, and that's what matters. Now are you coming in, or is somebody going to carry you?"

"I don't need carrying!" she spat. "I'm not a baby!"

That was ridiculous. Of course she was a baby. She still had blue eyes, and—except for Thea, who's a law unto herself—that means a kitten. I won't take insubordination, and it was past time Lottie was taught a few manners. I went forward very quickly, taking her by surprise, and picked her up. She squawked—very bad language—but I had my mouth too full of the scruff of her neck to reply, then she went limp, as good kittens do, and I carried her to the back door.

Willow and Tara barked, and Casper was still running around in circles.

Boss came and opened the door, and we all went in. Naturally I was the hero of the hour. Boss and Friend praised me extravagantly, and everyone was given extra biscuits and the cats were given a little milk each, especially Lottie, who still didn't know what the fuss was about. I didn't tell her, because she had too much sense of her own importance as it was. I would rather she didn't know the whole house was turned upside down looking for her. I would have told everyone to treat her coolly, if I hadn't known they would do that anyway.

It was only three days till Christmas, and Herbie and the other geese were still missing. And of course the Woofer

Wagon was still gone too. There was a great deal for us to do.

"Do you suppose the geese are in boxes somewhere?" Casper said hopefully.

I know the thieves had probably taken the geese to eat, and food often comes in boxes. It was a very grim thought.

"No!" I said sharply. We were lying around in our baskets in the kitchen. Boss had gone to bed. There were cats sitting on the table, but in the dark I wasn't sure who. I couldn't tell one black cat from another at this distance. Neither could Casper, which is a source of much embarrassment to him. He keeps mistaking Bertie for Boswell, which is a real problem because Boswell will play with him, whereas Bertie will give him a good swipe, claws out. Casper is very wary of Bertie, indeed.

Casper subsided into his blanket again.

"We've got to do something," one of the cats said. "Otherwise there'll be no Christmas."

Willow grunted. She grunts in her sleep, so she might not have meant anything.

"Who are you?" I asked. "I can't tell one black cat from another in the dark."

"I can't tell one box from another," Casper said irrelevantly. Except that it wasn't irrelevant, it was actually very clever.

I sat up, making everybody start to attention in case something was happening. "I couldn't tell one goose from another," I said loudly. I didn't say that I couldn't tell a goose at all, because I'm still not sure what they are . . . exactly.

"You could tell Herbie," Willow pointed out. "He has a sore foot."

"That's how to hide something!" I said impatiently. "Put it with a whole lot of other things the same!"

Then they understood.

"Of course!" Bertie agreed with enthusiasm. "Find other

geese, and Roddy's geese will be there . . . or they may be! Where do we find other geese?"

I had no idea, so I said nothing.

"I'll think about it," Willow replied, and went back to sleep.

In the morning as usual Boss came downstairs and let us all out. We went careering out of the back door, falling over each other, and nearly banged into the Woofer Wagon, sitting right where it should be in the drive.

Casper ran up to it and sniffed, then started to yip again, that high sound that goes right through your head.

Boss came to the back door, and this time she realized the Woofer Wagon was there, and she came out as well and walked all around it too. Then she went back in and telephoned Friend, even though it was pretty early.

After breakfast Boss and Friend went to look at it more closely. It is not the sort of car to examine for bumps or scratches, it has all the marks of an interesting life. But it was definitely worth looking at very closely indeed, and going over with the nose, to learn what we could of where it had been and who had taken it! That has to be very high on the list of terrible sins.

Boss and Friend found nothing broken. It was pretty muddy, but that washes off. Anyway, there's nothing wrong with mud.

Willow climbed inside as soon as she had the chance. That is where anything interesting would be. And she has the best nose. The next moment Tara was in it too, snuffling into everything with little hiccuping noises.

It wasn't long before Tara found a white feather.

"Pillows!" she said instantly. "And something else . . . it'll come to me in a minute what it is. And something horrible as well . . . something I really don't like at all." And she backed out very quickly, Willow after her.

"Well, what is it?" I demanded.

Nobody answered.

Casper went in and came out again, looking puzzled. "It's boys," he said. "That's what it is. It isn't all that horrible. In fact it's quite pleasant. It's the boys who tidy up Boss's garden."

"No that's not it," Tara argued. "I remember now . . . it's vets! It's sore places, stitches and prickles and things. It's things that hurt."

"It's boys," Casper repeated.

"It's Herbie's medicine," Willow said. "For his feet."

Bertie pushed past us and got into the Woofer Wagon. He likes riding in any car at all. He sniffed around, from the expression on his face not liking it a lot. He found another feather.

"Geese," he said uncertainly. He isn't sure what geese are either, but it was a nice piece of deduction.

"Herbie, anyway," I agreed.

"And boys," Tara added.

"You are quite right. So that means the boys took the Woofer Wagon and the geese." I was thinking hard what we should do about it.

"I'll go home and ask," Tara offered. And before I could tell her it was a waste of time—she's only got cats to talk to—she was gone.

We mooched around the garden thinking, and not coming up with anything. The boys had made it all tidy and it looked and smelled different, but there was some nicely turned earth, good for digging in.

Tara came back looking very pleased with herself, but then she's a Labrador, and it's built into them, like collies staring at people, and spaniels sitting in the water.

"We've got to rescue Herbie," she said. "That's our job! That's what we are for . . . rescuing."

"I know that!" What an unnecessary remark! We are all rescued, from something or other.

Tara never takes offense. That's a Labrador thing too.

"We can't tell Boss and Friend that," she said. "They don't have noses . . . well, not that they are any good. But they can see pretty well. I asked Thea and Pansy. They told me. Said to get something that the boys left behind in the garden—they're always dropping things and forgetting them—and put them in the Woofer Wagon. Then they'll realize!"

"What good is that?" Casper asked.

"If they catch the boys, then they'll catch the geese as well!" I told him.

He looked crestfallen. He should have thought of that himself.

"First we've got to find something," I instructed them all. "Spread around and go and look. We'll think what to do when we've got it."

It took quite a long time. I don't know how long because I didn't count. It was Willow who brought it back. It was a little piece of tin, round, with a picture on the front and a pin on the back. It smelled of boys, all right, and maybe Boss or Friend would know it was theirs and realize the truth . . . and then rescue Herbie and the others.

"Good," I said approvingly. "Now we've got to put it in the Woofer Wagon."

"They've closed the doors," Willow said exasperatedly. "You can open the back door of the house, but even you couldn't open one of these!"

"The window's open." Bertie looked at it, measuring it to see if he could squeeze through.

"What we need is a distraction," I told them. "No one must see Bertie put it there. Let's all go out on the road. That will make them all come after us."

"No, it won't," Tara argued. "They'll just shout at us!"

"Ignore them," I ordered.

She looked confused. I don't know why! She usually ignores them anyway.

Actually it worked very well. We had a good chase along the road and right around the corner toward Rockfield. It was a lot of fun. Boss and Friend were very cross, but no real harm came of it. We were shut inside, of course, but by that time Bertie was sitting on the kitchen table washing himself and looking smug.

"Well?" I demanded.

"Mission accomplished," he replied, without losing a lick.

Later the police came back, very pleased to see the crime had more or less solved itself. We very nearly got shut in again. We only managed to get out by pushing hard and squeezing through at the same time as Boss went out. Actually, you can do that nearly every time, with a little practice and a lot of insistence.

We helped the police, who seemed to appreciate us, and Willow found the little piece of colored tin, where Bertie had left it. She came out triumphantly and presented it to Boss, who suddenly looked very unhappy.

"Have you seen it before?" the policeman asked.

"Yes," Boss said quietly. "It belongs to one of the boys who was up here working in the garden."

"Are you certain?"

"Yes, I'm afraid so."

"Then we better go and have a talk with them," the policeman said grimly.

"I don't really want to press charges," Boss insisted.

"But we found feathers in there as well."

"Feathers?" He was surprised.

"Yes . . . white goose feathers. We think it may have been used to steal Roddy's geese. It was covered with mud. It's been off the road somewhere."

"I see. Well that's a different matter. Can't have livestock stolen."

"Will you let me know, please?" Friend asked. "One of the geese was a pet."

"Yes, of course we will." And they got into their car and drove off.

But it didn't turn out so easily. The police came back sometime later and said that they had seen the boys.

"They own up to taking the car," the man said with a frown. "And even to taking the geese, including the pet one. But they said they did it to rescue the geese because they were afraid Roddy was going to sell them for Christmas and they'd get eaten."

"So where are they?" Boss asked.

"Are they all right?" Friend added. "What about Herbie's foot?"

"I'm sure Roddy wouldn't press charges," Boss went on. "He isn't like that at all."

"He'd probably think it was quite funny, and like them for it," Friend said.

"But that's it." The policeman shook his head. "They haven't got the geese anymore. They say somebody else stole the geese from them!" He pursed his lips. "But that sounds like a tall story to me. I'll bet they sold them, and just didn't expect us to know who took the car."

"The one thing is, they don't have any money and haven't been seen to spend any in the last day or two," the policeman said. "Still . . . it is an unlikely story."

"Are you going to charge them?" Boss asked unhappily.

"Caution them for now," the policeman said. "Not enough proof. If we find a better trail we'll have to."

This really was developing very badly. Why did those stupid boys have to go and steal Herbie?

It was getting cold and beginning to snow. We said

goodbye to the police and all trooped back into the kitchen to sit by the stove and brood. Tara came too, since Friend and Boss wanted to sit and brood as well.

"I like the boys," Casper said, for once not bothering to stare out of the window to see if next door's dogs would show at the fence. "They talk to me . . . a lot."

"We all like them, more or less," I agreed. Actually I am rather wary of strangers, but I have more sense than Casper. He is not much more than a puppy.

Lottie was chasing a Ping-Pong ball around the floor and making a racket. Bertie boxed her ears for her as she went charging by him, and she took no notice at all, barely broke her stride.

"It's a lot more important to rescue Herbie." Humphrey had sneaked in somewhere and was licking his lips. "He'll be eaten if we don't."

"We must help." Willow sat up.

"I know that!" I replied. She is very irritating when she keeps repeating what we all know.

"Vets," Casper said loudly.

"What?"

"Vets," he repeated.

"You mean like Kenny, or Colm?" I asked.

"I suppose so. But vets."

Casper has never been to the real vet, but he is obsessed by them because he watches them on television everytime he can. The screen is covered with his nose marks. Boss has to keep wiping it clean.

"They know everything," he added.

Then I had a brilliant idea. "No they don't!" I contradicted. "But when you go to see them, there are usually lots of other cats and dogs and rabbits and things there. Between all of them . . . they will know . . . and we can ask them!"

"Wonderful!" Tara started banging her tail so wildly she

was told to stop it. She took no notice. "We'll go tomorrow morning. No . . . better . . . we'll go tonight, then we won't miss breakfast."

That is a disadvantage. Sometimes when going to the vet you get nothing to eat for ages before.

"You have to be sick to go to the vet," I pointed out.

"No, you don't," Bertie argued. "Sometimes you feel perfectly all right, and they take you in and poke needles into you."

"Kittens," I told him. "Not dogs. We all need to go. This is extremely important."

"Well, we'll pretend to be ill," Willow offered. "I can limp very well." She stood up and limped so dramatically she nearly fell over, just to illustrate.

We all tried limping on a succession of feet, but no one took the slightest notice.

Then we tried looking ill, but they just thought we were asleep.

"We've got to do better than this!" I said desperately. "Time is growing short! We're getting turkeys and hampers for everyone tomorrow, so Herbie may not live very long!"

Willow howled.

Casper copied her.

Tara stood up and trod on Willow, who started to cough.

That got their attention! Boss became really quite worried. It was a very good idea. I started to cough as well. Casper got so enthusiastic he nearly choked himself.

"We'd better take them to the vet," Boss said anxiously. "Do you think it's too late?"

"Not if we hurry," Friend said. "If we leave it, it will be Christmas and there'll be nobody there except for emergencies. Bertie's coughing as well, and now would be a good time to get Boswell his injections. He's the only one Colm didn't catch when he was up here."

I looked around and saw Boswell's black tail disappear

out of the cat flap. He's done that every time for two months now!

We all piled into the car—not the Woofer Wagon, the real car—and we set off to go to see Kenny, or Colm, whoever was there.

We raced along in the dark as far as the Tain turnoff, then down the low road, and picked up speed along the flats. It would have been nice to sing, but we were supposed to be ill, so I had to remind everyone not to. It was a pity. It was the ideal time and place.

We went over the humpbacked bridge and around the corner up the hill to Tain. The main street of the town was lit up with stars and wreaths, and of course all the shop windows and the ordinary lights. There seemed to be lots of cars and people out.

We turned left and went up to the other street, and up again to the vets. The car stopped and we all piled out, Friend carrying Bertie, who didn't like that much. He would have preferred to walk, but Boss was afraid he would get a fright and perhaps run away.

Inside, the waiting room was nice and warm. I looked around for what was important: other animals. What a relief! There were three dogs—a rottweiler, a greyhound, and a small white terrier. There was only one cat, a rabbit in a box, and a guinea pig. We all entered in a very good order and sat down.

Very quietly I explained the problem to the rottweiler.

"Geese?" he said thoughtfully. "I know geese. They are excellent to chase."

That didn't help at all. Lots of things are excellent to chase. I've seen people who should know better chasing their own tails. Lewis, our very old white cat, did it once at the top of the stairs. He caught it, and tied himself in a knot and rolled all the way down. But that is irrelevant. "Where

are they?" I asked. "We need to find Herbie, before anybody eats him."

The rottweiler was very apologetic, but he had no idea.

I asked the greyhound. She didn't know either.

It was the rabbit who interrupted. I thought it was
asleep, but apparently it wasn't.

"They live on farms," it said in a rather superior fashion.
"We've got lots of them, all white and gray. They make a
terrible noise, and they are very fierce."

"Do you have any with sore feet?" Casper asked eagerly.

The rabbit gave him a long stare. "I have no idea," it
replied at length. "I don't speak to geese."

"Where do you live?" I asked as civilly as possible.

"Down by the bridge," it said, and turned its back. I
think actually it wasn't very well, which was presumably
why it was here.

I thanked it, and looked at Casper, Willow, and Tara.

"We must go there," I said firmly. "It isn't very far. We
passed it on the way in. If Herbie is there, we should rescue
him."

"And all the others," Bertie added.

"Of course. But how do we get out of here? The door is
shut."

"Someone will come or go," Tara said. "When they do,
we'll all make a dash. Friend and Boss will chase after us,
and we'll all rescue Herbie." She looked very pleased with
herself.

It was an excellent plan. We all agreed, and sat down to
wait.

It wasn't long before the rabbit was called in, and somebody came out with a small box. Apparently there was a
mouse inside. She paid the bill and opened the door to leave.

"Now!" I yelled. "Charge!"

Nobody stands a chance when Tara charges. She's built

like a tank. She lunged at the door. The lady with the mouse was knocked sideways, screaming. I went racing after. Bertie shot between my legs, and Casper leaped right over the top of me. I do hate it when he does that! Willow brought up the rear.

We all went careering along the street and around the corner down to the main road. I didn't bother to look backward to make sure Boss and Friend were following. It was an absolute certainty. Anyway, I could hear the shouting all the way through the traffic, cars screeching to a halt as we flew across the road, men and women calling out, children cheering us on.

There were car horns blaring and somebody roaring with laughter, and music playing. They always do that at Christmas.

We all raced out of the town, down the hill toward the humpbacked bridge, ears flying, tails streaming out behind us, Casper barking with excitement. Even Bertie was along in there somewhere.

We reached the farm and tore up the driveway and into the open space near the barn.

There was a terrible honking and squawking going on, as if somebody were very angry indeed—or very frightened. We all scrambled around in the dark for several minutes, not really sure of anything. Then there was a glare of lights as two cars came along the drive and stopped, shining on us.

We were in the middle of a lot of very big white birds, bigger than chickens even, a lot bigger than Bertie, who looked very nervous indeed. Actually I was glad Tara was with us, and Bertie went and stood very close to her.

"Courage!" I hissed, especially to Casper, who was obviously very apprehensive indeed.

Willow sat down, which was brave of her. Either that or her legs gave way.

Boss and Friend got out of the first car, then Kenny right behind them. The policeman got out of the second car and came over, shining his flashlight around, beyond the light from the cars.

"What on earth's going on here?" he asked, his voice rising high. "There's a cat here! And half a dozen dogs—and heaven knows how many geese!"

The policeman walked in among the big birds and bent down to look more closely at one of them, who just stood there, not in the least bothered.

"I think this might be Herbie," he said cheerfully. "He's still got a bit of ointment on his foot. We seem to have found the lost geese—at least the dogs seem to have."

Kenny came over and bent down as well. "Yes, that's Herbie," he said with a smile. "He doesn't look too bad."

There was a noise over by the barn, and another light appeared, then a man came around the corner looking very angry.

"It's Roddy's friend!" Willow said to me. "He must be the one who took Herbie and the others."

Boss and Friend and Kenny and the policeman must have had the same idea, because they all turned to him.

"Are these your geese, sir?" the policeman asked.

First the man said no, then he said yes, then he said he wasn't sure. We got back into the car with Boss and Friend, and Kenny, who took Herbie with him to put some more ointment on his foot.

Everybody told us we were very clever, and Kenny gave us all biscuits from a large sack behind the counter, and gave Bertie some tiny little ones for cats. Nobody said anything about us having run off.

Herbie sat down on the counter with one foot sticking out.

"So that's a goose," Casper said, staring up at him. "I always thought it was."

I didn't bother to ask him what he meant by that. It was time to go home. If we were lucky, tomorrow we might go to the beach. I led the way out.

"Happy Christmas, Goose!" Casper called over his shoulder.

Nancy Pickard won back-to-back Agatha Awards for her novels, Bum Steer *and* I.O.U., *featuring foundation official Jenny Cain, and also received an Agatha for Best Short Story for "Out of Africa." Her new book is* The Whole Truth, *with a new character, true crime writer Marie Lightfoot. This story describes a startling aftermath of a near-death experience . . .*

Lucky Devil

Nancy Pickard

It's not fair.

Except for the beautiful part, *none* of what happened to me is fair.

I've tried to grasp whatever larger, cosmic reason there may be for it all, but high-flown philosophy is not my forte. "Josie's of a practical nature," my mother used to say to me, and heaven knows she was right about that. If I am anything, it is down-to-earth. At the moment, I am damnably so.

My name, as you may know from newspaper accounts,

193

is Josephine Taylor. I am sixty-three years old, widowed for so many years it feels as if I was never married. I live alone, I am a cashier at a bank. I don't suppose it takes an Einstein to read that description and get a pretty good idea of me as I am. And yes, I'm a bit of a fuss-budget. I've always liked things to be logical and orderly, from my checkbook to the books I check out of the library. I suppose if you want to read a little loneliness between the lines, I can hardly argue. It is true that somehow the days of my life have always seemed longer than the chronology of my years. In my forties I began to sense the inevitable dying of my cells, the daily, dusty walk toward death. My family are long-lived, however; I felt sure I would follow the example of my hardy parents and not die until my eighties.

Imagine my surprise when it happened sooner than that!

Medical death, they call it, and they termed my survival a miracle. No doubt you've heard similar stories, though none, I'll wager, quite like mine. Perhaps you have even experienced it yourself, but not as I did, I feel safe to say. As for skeptics, I would remind them that it was I, not they, who experienced it, and so they may not presume to speak for me. I know I was truly dead, with no qualifying adjectives like "medical" to soften it for our rational minds. I *died* on that mild September night, and now I am regrettably alive.

I was murdered.

"Lovely weather," my neighbor called out to me on that fateful Thursday evening when I stepped out of our apartment building for my nightly stroll. It was, indeed, a lovely twilight, soft and warm as only certain autumn nights can be, with a cloudless sky turning gracefully to a vast, dark blue.

"Hello, Esther," I greeted her, and then her dog. "Captain."

She was seated on a bench, with the big yellow Labrador lying at her feet. At the sound of my voice, he wagged his tail. His leash was loosely wrapped around Esther's left hand, which was no guarantee that she could hold him back if he decided to bolt. He's a friendly creature, but he has been known to charge pedestrians, so I always gave him a wide berth.

"I hope you'll be careful, Josie, dear. You'll walk under streetlights, won't you?"

"I'll be careful."

I was not afraid to walk alone in our neighborhood, but it was comforting to know there was at least one person in the world who would notice if I failed to return before dark.

I felt so weary that night. My shoulders ached and I probably slumped a bit. No doubt my head was down and my eyes were looking at my feet as I shuffled away the dreariness of the day.

"You were an inviting target," police officers told me afterward. "You were just the sort of person they like to prey upon: an older woman, not paying any attention to where she's going or who's around her."

And then, to top it off, I had my purse with me, as I always do, because it holds my keys. I also like to carry a little change in case I decide to stop at the Baskin-Robbins for a caramel sundae.

"Really, Mrs. Taylor," my lawyer chided me later. "You might as well have worn a sign that said 'Rob Me.' "

Perhaps the "experts" were not, after all, surprised by the assault on me. But the victim certainly was. Oh, it was so quick, so startling, so utterly terrifying!

He jumped out at me, grabbed the strap of my purse and tried to jerk it away from me. When he did that, he jerked

my arm, too, catching me off balance. I began to fall. At
that point everything slowed down. Slowly, I fell, so slowly
it seemed I had time to study the cement in the pavement
below me, to see its cracks, its gritty surface rising to meet
me. All the while, I *knew* with a sickening awareness that
this was going to be a very bad fall. I would be hurt; it
would damage me.

But it didn't hurt at all.

It merely killed me.

Instantly, as my head struck the sidewalk, I felt a
tremendous *whoosh,* as if I were being sucked out of my
body, into the air above me. I'm sure you've heard similar
reports, so I will not bore you with the familiar details, except to confirm that it is true what you have heard. Suddenly I was above myself, watching people running toward
me and then bending over me. I saw the backs of their
heads. I saw my own face! What surprises me even now is
that I felt such loving sympathy for that poor pale woman
lying so pitifully there on the pavement, with her blood
trickling into the street.

Poor dear Josephine, I thought, tenderly.

I hovered there above. I watched an ambulance arrive
and paramedics rush my limp body into it. They seemed
outwardly calm, inwardly frantic.

"Get a move on!" the eldest of them muttered to himself.

I wanted to tell them not to bother.

A tall thin man I recognized from the neighborhood
shook his head and looked touchingly dejected. "It's too
late for her," I heard him say, and I wanted to comfort him.

Don't be sad, I wanted to say.

I even watched my assailant run away, and observed him
being pursued by strangers who had come to my aid. They
yelled at him, they were furious on my behalf. I started to

follow them, to see if they'd catch him, but suddenly I didn't have time for that. Quicker than an instant I was gone from there, sucked further from earth. Down a tunnel I fell like Alice, down and down. I promised I wouldn't bore you with the details, but it is important for me to tell just a little more of what happened next. I became abruptly aware of a wonderful, bright light, and I tumbled into it. And suddenly everything was beautiful, peaceful, happy, more lovely than anywhere on earth, more peaceful than the stillest pool. I felt more happy than the happiest day that anyone has ever known.

I have died, I thought with wonder.

But then I felt a pulling again, as if forces were trying to suck me back into the world I had left. I fought it. I wept, crying, "No, please, I don't want to go back."

The next thing I knew I was hovering over my body again. This time I was hooked up to machines that registered no life in me. Doctors and nurses pummeled my thin body as if they could pound it back to life.

No! I tried to yell at them. *I won't come back!*

But I couldn't resist the gravity of existence. I whirled back into my body. Then came awful pain. I knew I was alive again. I opened my eyes.

"She's alive!" they shouted joyously, as if they'd done me a favor.

I wept for days.

There have been so many thousands of reports of after-death experiences that no one doubted my travelogue of heaven. They were interested. They called in their friends to hear it. A few of them took notes.

It was only when I insisted I had been murdered that I encountered resistance.

"What do you mean, he murdered you?" The police

smiled at the very idea. "He can't very well have killed you, not if you're here to complain about it. Now can he, Mrs. Taylor?"

My lawyer said in her condescending way, "He can't be tried for murder. You're alive, you see."

This attitude is illogical of them. If they believe I died, how can they deny the corollary truth of my homicide?

A judge was sympathetic but curt.

"Be grateful that he'll wind up in jail at all, Mrs. Taylor," he advised me. "You are fortunate there were witnesses to apprehend him. He'll be punished for assaulting and robbing you, you may be sure of that."

But I am not grateful.

Having experienced a beautiful world of truth and justice, I know the boy should face the rightful consequences of his earthly actions. He is old enough to be tried as an adult for murder. This is a death penalty state. If people would only behave rationally, the boy could be given a fresh start in life, by dying.

"Even if I wanted to prosecute him," the prosecutor has said to me, "there is no such law on the books. Our society has no provision for dealing with the murderers of victims who don't *stay* dead."

He seemed to find that amusing.

The injustice of it all weighs upon my mind as I heal in my body. It all seems so unfair to the boy and me. He will only continue to degenerate here on earth. As for me, I am cheated of that paradise I was privileged to glimpse. I miss it terribly, as one might miss a beloved home; I long with all of my soul to return to it. Before I was murdered, life seemed barely endurable. Now it feels more barren than ever; now I cannot tolerate the thought of the years that lie before me until my next death. I want so badly that bliss which I tasted for that sweet short time.

Others have come back from such experiences claiming they were assigned a mission in life.

I was told nothing like that.

But I believe I do have a special mission.

The boy is out on bail. He has already returned to this neighborhood. Through the week I have unobtrusively observed his comings and goings. I am waiting for the right moment to present itself. I have seen him swagger, I have watched him brag to his friends. I am hopeful for him.

I plan to help him tonight.

He must be alone.

It must be fully dark outside, with no one near us.

I will approach him, holding in front of me one of the two small guns that my father left to me.

"You?" the boy will say, smirking until he sees the gun and the loving determination on my face. "Hey!"

"Stand still," I will order him.

Then I will take the second gun from the pocket of my cardigan sweater. I will hold it out to him and say, "Take this."

He will look puzzled and obscurely frightened, but he will take the gun.

"It's loaded," I will assure him.

He will begin to smile, possibly even raising his gun to me.

"What the hell?" he may ask, for the last time.

"I want you to kill me," I will direct him. "I will count to five. If you don't shoot me by the time I get to five, I will shoot you. One . . ."

He will look blank, stupid.

"Two."

I will aim at his heart.

"You're crazy!" he will exclaim.

But by the time I reach the count of four, he will shoot me in order to save himself. As I die, my little gun will fall to the ground. The boy will run away, but that won't matter. Everyone will know whom to suspect in my death.

The prosecutor will arrest the boy, who will attempt to tell his strange story, which no one will believe. They will say, "That poor lady carried a gun to protect herself against you. You killed her to keep her from testifying against you." Then they will try and convict him for his true crime: murder. And at last he will be privileged to face the heavenly consequences of his crime.

It isn't fair!

Nothing happened as I planned it.

Tonight, when I handed the gun to the boy, he looked bewildered, just as I knew he would, and he looked vaguely frightened, too.

"I will count to five," I told him.

It was then that the big yellow dog came bounding out of nowhere, lunging playfully at my legs. I fell forward against the boy. It was *my* gun that went off, firing at him, rather than his gun firing at me.

Oh, the lucky young devil!

"Justifiable," the police have assured me. "Obviously he was trying to silence your testimony. Of course, you had to protect yourself."

Of course.

And so it is I who am still alive and the boy who is dead. Perhaps even now he is savoring the bliss of that heaven where all is forgiven. I'm sure he thanks me.

I have not given up hope for myself, however.

There will be other ways of going home again, and perhaps some other boy to whom I may give a fresh start.

Elizabeth Daniels Squire's memory-challenged but resourceful sleuth Peaches Dann appears in seven novels, including Where There's a Will *and* Forget about Murder, *and her Agatha Award–winning short story, "The Dog Who Remembered Too Much," in* Malice Domestic 4. *In this story, Peaches stumbles across something more in the compost heap than mulch . . .*

Down the Garden Path

Elizabeth Daniels Squire

Almost every Saturday morning, right after I see the TV news and read the paper, I take a walk, and I stop down the road and hear about the adventures of Mimi's imaginary friend named Pompadori. Pompadori rode tigers and elephants when the circus was here in Asheville, and among other amazing accomplishments, she knew how to fly right over our mountains.

I have to admit that after the road-rage incidents, school shootings, and employees gone berserk with guns that filled the media, I found that Mimi's gentle fantasy was nice. She would come to the edge of her lawn under a maple tree and we'd chat.

But last Saturday I was startled to hear that Pompadori had found a body in the compost heap. A body? Boy, I thought, something must be truly upsetting this kid for her imagination to come up with a body.

Mimi is just five years old, and one of those kids you find yourself pulling for. She has presence.

She stood there by the road in her cheerful T-shirt with hearts and a teddy bear on it, denim overalls and mismatched socks. I noticed her eyes. They're gray, and they seemed sad and wise and naive all at once. The big black dog named Fritsie, who was usually with her, was nowhere in sight. Had something happened to Fritsie? I waited to see what Mimi would tell me.

"Mama says I make up stories and tell lies, Miz Peaches, but Grandma says that I'm her angel," she said. I'd met Grandma. She's a salt-of-the-earth type.

"Stories don't have to be lies," I told Mimi. "Some people get paid for making up stories."

She'd smiled at that. But then her forehead wrinkled with worry. "Mama drinks a magic potion," she told me. "Mama gets sleepy." I wondered if that was a fanciful way of saying her mother, Mabel, drank too much.

I hardly knew Mabel. I remembered her name because it's like *Maybe* plus *L*. And maybe she could be as colorful and rotten as neighborhood gossip said. *Maybe* she did raise *L*. But *Maybe* not. A would-be pop singer, I heard, but not successful enough to cut the mustard; divorced, an alcoholic and a nymphomaniac with a nasty temper. So said my unfavorite neighbor, Nina the Whiner. I wait and believe what I see.

Right after she moved in last year, Mabel had contacted us neighbors and offered to trade organic vegetables for our grass clippings, vegetable peels, and other compostables. Four of us, including Nina, took her up on it.

But Mabel never came to collect these herself. She'd hired a gorgeous young man named Monk, about twenty years old, to work in her garden, and he came by once a week for the pickup. Maybe he was Mabel's lover. Nina the Whiner had suggested that. If I was thirty years younger and not happily married, I might have been tempted.

Monk didn't just rely on his amazing good looks: good bones, sexy muscles, glowing skin, luxurious hair. He was magnificent even in old cutoffs and a T-shirt and high-topped black work shoes, picture perfect, except his eyes were appraising and greedy and needy at the same time. Those eyes bothered me. Otherwise, he was all charm.

Just yesterday I had thanked him for the beautiful squash and cucumbers and beans and more that Mabel sent. So I wanted to have kind thoughts of Monk and also of Mabel.

But today, when Mimi took hold of my arm, I could feel she was trembling. I could feel alarm.

"There's a foot in the compost, and Mama is sick, and bad Mrs. Broken Face yelled at Monk," she said. Strange words from a child who looked as gentle and pretty as an angel on a Christmas card.

I knew "Mrs. Broken Face" was our neighbor Annie, who has a birthmark.

I call her Annie the Fannie because she is nastily divorced and fading pretty and she switches her tail like a high sign. She comforts herself with men. Monk delivered vegetables to her, too . . .

Mimi took hold of my arm again and pulled. "Mama is sick." Mimi's eyes said *Help!*

So I let her pull me around in back of the white clapboard house onto the stone terrace overlooking the vegetable garden, and there sat her mama, Mabel, drinking tea—Mabel, with slightly disheveled long red hair and slightly bloodshot eyes. Behind her, just beyond the terrace, were rows of beautifully-cared-for shining red tomatoes and yellow squash and dark green kale and much more, in softly turned rich black soil. Certainly no one with such a garden could be too bad.

Mabel leaned back in her white wicker chair and nervously adjusted a designer denim jacket. She raised her eyes and stared at me as if I was a ghost. "What the hell are you doing here?" she asked. "You're the third one."

Behind her, down at the end of the garden, was the large compost heap with my grass clippings and vegetable peels and such included. One end was hidden behind a row of pole beans.

Mabel poured herself some tawny liquid from a large brown teapot. I realized it wasn't tea. More like scotch whiskey, even if she did pour it in a cup.

I sat down. Mabel took a gulp of the liquid.

I told her how I enjoyed the vegetables. Then I asked, "I'm the third what? The third one to visit you this morning?" Strain rose sinews in her neck and lined her face. She didn't answer.

Mimi twisted her hands together as she sat in a small wicker chair just her size. She said, "Mrs. Big-Foot yelled, too."

Mimi has her own names for our neighbors. She meant self-righteous Laurie down the road. Laurie is large, like one of those great big Japanese wrestlers, and she does have big feet. She minds everybody else's business with a heavy hand. I knew she'd called social services to try to get Mimi removed from her mama. Yet Laurie's own daughter, Laura Sue, is a wild kid in spite of Laurie's best efforts. "If that Monk makes a pass at Laura Sue, I'll give him what-for!" she'd said. Yes, heavy-handed. I, myself, called her

Run-over-'em Laurie since *lorry* is what the Brits call a truck. Nicknames are a favorite memory trick.

"Was Laurie here this morning?" I asked Mabel tactfully. Something here was ugly.

"Nobody was here!" she cried. She smelled afraid, a sweetish smell that mixed strangely with the scent of whiskey.

Mimi held onto her chair tight. She was scared, too, but in a different way. I couldn't quite put my finger on the difference. "Monk said he'd make me a paper bird today," she said. "But he's not here."

"Monk tells every damn person what they want to hear," Mabel cried out, as if she couldn't bear it.

I knew it could be true. Monk had my number. "I hear you've written a book," he'd told me, so very sweetly as he handed me a bunch of parsley. "All about memory tricks. That's wonderful! I have trouble remembering names and numbers, myself. But I have a trick that always works. I learned it from my mother," he'd said, as if that made it a personal favor for him to tell me. "Mom's a surgical nurse. If she absolutely has to remember something during an operation, she puts a bandage on her hand and writes on the bandage. I just write on myself." He'd held up his left hand and glanced at me for my approval.

"That way I don't have to stop and look in my little book," he'd said, pulling a black notebook out of his pocket. "I write poetry," he'd said, as if that explained the notebook. A pretty drawing of a bunch of flowers fell out of it, primitive but eye-catching. He'd grinned. "The Kid drew that: Mimi. She's a real little artist. She did it just for me," he said proudly.

I'd thanked him for that write-on-the-hand memory trick as warmly as he'd plainly needed. Need can be dangerous.

Now I looked around Mabel's garden. I knew that Monk

worked Saturdays. So why wasn't he here? This man who wanted admiration even from a little child.

Mimi said Annie and Laurie had been here, yet her mother denied it. Hey, they were both members of the compost club. And Pompadori said there was a man in the compost heap. Pompadori who wasn't even real. Somehow, what I was hearing almost fit together in a nightmare, but not quite. At least one member of the compost club had been left out. Nina the Whiner. Nina whose husband traveled. She complained about that nonstop. He was a smart man. He'd managed to get them a phone number that even I could remember. Our local exchange plus 5555. Said it helped him when he did business at home.

I'm not sure why, but I asked: "Was Nina here this morning?"

"No!" Mabel cried. "That woman . . . is a slut. I wouldn't let her even . . . come in my yard!"

Mimi ignored that. No comment about Nina from Pompadori. "Fritsie found the shoe," she said urgently. "Mama put Fritsie in the cellar."

So that was why Mimi's big black dog was nowhere in sight.

"Mimi heard my brother," Mabel said, enunciating slowly. "My stupid brother . . . who eats fast food . . . said that I am such a fanatic about my vegetables . . . that when I die . . . I'll leave my body to a compost heap . . . So Mimi made up one of her stories."

I prayed that was true.

Mabel was drinking her whiskey at an alarming rate. Two butterflies danced around us. She didn't even seem to see them.

I turned to Mimi. "If I go down to the compost heap and look and I come back and tell you that there is no man in that shoe, will you believe me?"

All she said was, "Please look!" She was trembling again.

"You stay with your mama. She needs you," I said. So Mimi went over and stood close to her mother, frowning with worry when Mabel began to cry. From whiskey self-pity? I hoped it was that.

I walked past Mabel, who was still gulping her "tea," past rows of glowing purple eggplant with their peppery smell, several kinds of tomatoes, bush beans, parsley, dill, and cilantro. I picked a sprig of dill as I passed and crushed it and sniffed the wonderful sour odor that spoke of pickles that could be. I looked off at the blue-green mountains. I didn't want to hurry to confront—what?

And I had an odd thought that whatever was wrong might be the fault of our wonderful mountains. You see, Asheville is a place where people come with the impression that they can fulfill their dreams. Maybe it's the view of mountains, one behind another, or something in the air. Creative people flourish here and always have. Thomas Wolfe wrote about this place. Bela Bartok wrote music here. Potters, artists, writers, musicians, and new-age healers fill the hills and hollers.

But unless you can bring your job with you, it's hard to get the kind of work you want here. And in this place of high hopes, the ones who don't blossom can get bitter. I was the only one in our compost club who wasn't bitter. An odd concentration, but that's how it was. And bitter can lash out. Was that somehow related to a dead man in the compost—if there was one? Or was the dead man only the fantasy of a lonely little girl's imaginary friend?

The compost, in its man-sized weathered wood box, stood just past the tall row of Romano pole beans. The end of the box I could see did not sprout a shoe. Good. But the compost seemed disturbed, with the bright new clippings unevenly mixed with the dark rotted old. I walked closer. And there at the other end of the heap was a black shoe, really a work boot. And, Lord help us, it was like the ones Monk wore. It stuck out of the heap of organic stuff in the box, ominous and ugly. I felt cold in the bright sun. The boot was sole outward. I knew the wearer could be under the tossed salad of new peels and clippings and black rotted compost. I shuddered. On the ground by the box was a shovel with bits of compost clinging to the business end. There was also something brown that could have been dried blood on one edge.

I walked back to Mimi and leaned down and kissed her on the top of the head. Her hair smelled fresh like new mown grass.

"I didn't lie," she said.

"No," I told her sadly. "You didn't lie."

I put my hand on Mabel's shoulder, trying to pull her to enough sobriety to hear what I said next. "I'm going to call Mimi's grandma to come get her," I said, "because the best thing Mimi can do for you and for herself is to be safe and well, and I'm also going to have to call the police."

The shock cleared Mabel's eyes, at least for a moment. I didn't know what to expect. Hysterics? More denial? I braced myself.

She took hold of my hand, and for one moment a look of raw anguish twisted her face. She said the last thing I expected. "Thank you.

"Go," she said to Mimi. "I want you to go." Then she raised her cup, which she had just filled, and downed it to the last drop. Her head fell forward onto her arms.

Mimi came with me reluctantly, looking back over her shoulder every minute, but she came. She showed me how to punch one button on the phone to get Grandma. I just said, "This is a neighbor. There's an emergency here. Please come get Mimi."

Grandma didn't even pause to ask questions. She just said, "I'll be there in five minutes."

I suggested that Mimi go get Fritsie from the basement. She said she'd get her suitcase, too. It was still packed from the last visit to her grandma.

As soon as she was gone, I called the police. I gave the address and said there seemed to be a dead man in the compost heap.

The dispatcher said, "If this is a joke, ma'am . . ."

I said I wished it was a joke and gave him my name.

I went upstairs and I admit I was nosy. I checked Mabel's bedroom with the unmade four-poster bed and the picture of a smiling Monk, framed on the dresser. Also another picture of Monk and Mabel together, holding up some huge tomatoes. Mabel smiled and her eyes were hopeful. Also there were two shirts that looked like his hanging in the closet. Yes, score one for Nina the gossip.

When I came back, Mimi was in the front hall by a red suitcase. She was hugging Fritsie hard. Obviously Mimi knew something was terribly wrong, but she said, "Grandma is coming," and smiled. Her grandmother was at the door almost by the time she'd said it.

Mimi said, "Grandma, I found a dead man in the compost heap," and she ran to her grandmother's arms for shelter.

I said, "I believe the police are about to arrive."

Grandma put her arms tight around Mimi. "My angel," she said. "You'll be safe with me.

"When you get a chance, call me," she said to me, giving me a card with her number. Her whole aim was obviously to get Mimi away as fast as possible, and to upset her as little as possible. A wise woman.

Before they could leave, I gave Mimi a quick hug. "Angels are strong," I said.

Luckily the first policeman who came was a friend of

mine. The one I call Mustache because he has one. I led Mustache toward the compost heap, past Mabel, who seemed to be sleeping, head still down, led him to the man-sized weathered wood box, just past those Romano pole beans. Mustache inspected the boot and shovel, pulled out his cellular phone and called for backup.

We stood away from the box, where he could keep an eye on Mabel and the compost all at once, though she appeared to be passed out.

Mustache asked me what I'd seen and heard, and I told him what had gone on in this house since I arrived. I guess I'm pretty good at that—after all, I'm a reporter now, even if my weekly paper is in the next county. Then he asked, "So what do you really think happened?"

Thank goodness Mustache doesn't resent the fact that sometimes, partly by luck, I figure out the answer where a murder is concerned. Actually, I surprise myself.

"I won't be sure what happened here," I said, "until you uncover the man whose foot is in that boot and I see what's written on his left hand."

Mustache did a double take. "But how do you know there's writing if you haven't seen the body?"

"Just a hunch, based on a remembering trick." I told him about Monk and his mother in the operating room. Monk who was beyond hope from any operation.

I figured the left hand in the compost heap would show whether three women killed Monk, or whether it was four.

When the backup team arrived it seemed to take forever to photograph the scene, then carefully uncover the body. Yes, it was poor Monk. I identified him and wished he'd died some more poetic way. Poor Monk who needed to be admired—I wished he hadn't been draped with rotting lettuce, a huge gash on his head stuck with bits of rotted vegetable in the dried blood.

At last his left hand was free and clear and wiped off. I

recognized the number written on it. Yes, it ended with 5555.

"Four women killed him," I told Mustache.

He blinked with surprise.

"So why did Mabel lie?" I mused out loud. "And say nobody came here this morning? And even accuse her daughter of being a liar?"

Mustache grinned. "You're going to tell me."

"Because," I said, "Mabel knew Annie and Laurie were links in the chain that led to murder." Then I explained what I believed took place. "Poor Monk needed to be admired so badly," I said, "that he did or said whatever you wanted. He said he liked your book or he said he loved you. Whatever. Mabel wanted him to be her lover. Exclusive rights. After all, he worked for her. Her neighbor Annie wanted the same thing, and Laurie's daughter was after him, I think." I sighed and thought how handsome but how young he'd been. "I don't think he knew how to handle all that. So first Annie came and told him off in front of Mabel. Perhaps he broke a date. Something like that." I could picture just how angry Mabel got when she learned of the Annie connection. "Then Laurie accused him of chasing her daughter, which made Mabel madder.

"The last straw must have been when poor Mabel saw our neighbor Nina's phone number written on his hand, and figured there was something going on between Monk and Nina.

"Three rages at a man who desperately needed admiration was more than he could bear. I bet he said 'I quit.' "

"Which was his right," Mustache sighed.

"Which added to Mabel's drunken rage. She hit him with the shovel, probably didn't mean to kill him, then was too drunk to get the body far, so she buried it in the compost heap. I don't think Mimi saw him killed, or she would have been even more upset than she was. Thank God for that. She must have been out front playing with the dog.

"Then Mabel was also too drunk to know what to do when Mimi discovered the shoe."

Mustache grinned. I don't know why I amuse him so. "I'll be interested to see," he said, "if our investigation comes to the same conclusion."

Later, as I read the story in the paper about poor Monk who'd been hit over the head with a shovel and buried in the compost heap, I was profoundly sorry.

And basically I'd been right. Rage did it. Rage, the great twentieth-century sport. A curse in our times. Rage that could invade an office or a school, or even a beautiful garden.

I prayed Mimi would find her way to a world without rage. I hoped that imagination, grown strong as her refuge, could help her make up stories, just to have fun.

Murder Is on the Menu
at the Hillside Manor Inn
Bed-and-Breakfast Mysteries by
MARY DAHEIM
featuring Judith McMonigle Flynn

Award-Winning Author

CAROLYN HART

THE HENRIE O MYSTERIES

DEATH IN LOVERS' LANE
0-380-79002-5/$6.50 US/$8.50 Can

DEATH IN PARADISE
0-380-79003-3/$6.50 US/$8.50 Can

DEATH ON THE RIVERWALK
0-380-79005-X/$6.50 US/$8.99 Can

THE DEATH ON DEMAND MYSTERIES

YANKEE DOODLE DEAD
0-380-79326-1/$6.50 US/$8.50 Can

WHITE ELEPHANT DEAD
0-380-79325/$6.50 US/$8.99 Can